ALSO BY DOUGLAS WOOLF.

The Hypocritic Days, 1955
Fade Out, 1959
Wall to Wall, 1961
Signs of a Migrant Worrier, 1965
Ya! & *John-Juan*, 1971
Spring of the Lamb, 1972

Douglas Woolf

ON US

Black Sparrow Press • Santa Barbara • 1977

LIBRARY OF CONGRESS CATALOGING IN PUBLICATION DATA

Woolf, Douglas.
    On us.

    I. Title.
PZ4.W91230n   [PS3573.O646]   813'.5'4   76-52385
ISBN 0-87685-285-1
ISBN 0-87685-284-3 pbk.

For Sandy

The first third of this book was written in the winter and spring of Wales, 1970, the rest in the late winter and spring of Minnesota, 1974.

ON US

ONE

Walking George thought oh ho, fly *fly*, as the bug toiled heavily overhead, for it had nowhere in Hell to go. He himself was on his way to work, with a promise of trees with leaves above, in winter yet. He had checked on Sunday, in the expiring Chev: arbutus and evergreen! Retired groundskeeper for 20-acre estate must know trees five mornings per week, the ad had read. He had taken Sunday off, for he did not *have* to work this week. No, he had spent his leisure backing Miss Palsey three crooked blocks to Bud's Garage. This had required some recklessness, for she was in danger of dropping her rear end along the way, perhaps in front of Livingston's Electronic Auto Clinic and Repair, Inc. With all the cops around, plus God knew how many hanging overhead, there would have been no choice. Thanks to her, at Bud's, he still did not have to work this week. No need to mention that to the new boss, of course. Nor that he was far from retired, was in fact always on the comeback trail. Glancing at the persistent sun, it occurred to him that a retired groundskeeper who needed work would apply in the morning hours. Thus he thought to waylay a bus.

He did not sit on the wooden bench, with the maimed spider there, nor look long at it. Someone had lately carved that out with a switchblade or pocket knife. Araneida swastika. Boys will be boys, end men. He raised his eyes, not so much skyward as heavenward, avoiding both the satellites and the sun. Why *look* for trouble, as the saying went. This was a superstition of his no doubt, hardly a necessary precaution yet. Phase One was operational, certainly, but they had not perfected it. Now here came Phase Two to rend the sky, and there was no doubting that: he looked down at once. By the

9

time their roar hit the back of his head with half its maximum force, they had developed their full-face photographs, transmitted them. Time to start looking for cover, before Phase Three arrived. Even as he looked, there came the saving bus! Its driver seemed bent on finding cover too; he had taken his dark glasses off. Or was he on strike? His vehicle was empty, his name-box blank. Ah, he was lost. Stopped at the corner, he peered left and right, peered again, then back to George. Shaking his head perplexedly, he swung the door.

George smiled in thanks. "Does this bus run south?"

"South? Get in!"

"Good!"

"How far south?"

"Near Mount Holyoke. I'll point it out."

Grunting the driver engaged his gears. Now, with a direction in mind, he drove hard ahead, scarcely glancing left or right. George sat close behind his back, by way of reassurance and encouragement, perhaps advice. No need for that, as it turned out. Phase Three was on to them. This inspired driver was dedicated to outrunning a bug, what with the road all downhill ahead. Did a bug have any advantage up there to compare with that? Did its pilot see that cloud down south? There must be all kinds of air pockets inside of that; did he want to find himself perched all askew on a telephone pole? Did he care to run into Mount Rainier? What did he know of the country beyond—Oregon, California, Nevada—had he filed a flight plan for that? Was he cleared for México? Did he want to precipitate an international incident? No, best he should turn back at once, return to port and file his report, before he reached the Point of No Return.

George hated to spoil such sport, but they had already sailed two blocks beyond Mount Holyoke. "This will do nicely, friend," he called, tapping the tense, hunched shoulder in front of him.

The driver stood on his brakes, brought his vehicle to a shuddering stop. Through the front window they watched the bug flailing the sudden vacuum created by them. Quickly it got hold of itself, using its sound-waves to steady it. The driver punched open his door. "Mount Holyoke!"

"Thanks!" George called, jumping out as the door swung

10

closed. The impatient driver was too busy to wave, but they were friends. His bus leapt forward, taking the bobbing bug along with it. George stood alone, regaining his breath in a peaceful cloud of smoke. When that began to thin, he headed quickly uphill toward trees. Those were arbutus and evergreen, all right, enclosed in an eight-foot fence, rusted, spiked. George aimed for the gate.

On the run he took a quick shot of the sun, for that gate looked shut. Not only shut but chained, padlocked. It would take two men with a crowbar to pick that lock. He thought to leave a note in the keyhole for his boss—"Sorry to have missed you!"—but had no paper large enough; such a keyhole begged for a book. A realist, he quickly saw his only choice: leave those lovely trees to grow an extra day, go home and write. Tomorrow catch an earlier bus. His driver had tried hard for him, had done his very best, and he had not known that George did not have to work this week.

To the north was a bit of haze or mist, he set his sights on that. If he hurried, perhaps home would be enwrapped in it. Once there had been a fog for four days and nights: in all that time, not one buzz from a bug, the fog horns had cheered themselves hoarse. At least there was comfort in such memories, and hope. He found himself walking well, his stride relaxed and free. But, even now, something in the air sought to pin him down. At first it reached him more as vibration than sound, an almost supersonic contradiction of the freedom he felt. His natural first thought was of a new phase coming up. If such was the case, they had not perfected it, for now above the monotonous beat could be heard a cloppety-clop. That was a horse. It could be clearly seen ahead, thin and piebald, bearing a plump equestrian on top. Jouncing up there, she gripped her reins and a flagpole together in both her hands, in advance of her troops, ten or twelve little boys in blue shirts and red caps. This "phase" was a ragged one, but much meant. The boys carried rifles, and they were scowling. Approaching George they turned eyes right, chanting—yelling—their cadence out: Your LEFT right LEFT . . . Your LEFT right LEFT . . . . . . LEFT . . . . . . LEFT . . . . . . LEFT . . . Snarled in her flapping nylon stars and stripes, their obese leader looked fiercely down on him. George waved and hurried on his way.

11

He had a detour in mind, on less trafficked roads, through a less prosperous neighborhood which the late leaf fall exposed. Here were almost as many unpruned trees as flag and other poles. Vegetable gardens lay in decay where might have been neat winter lawns. Scarecrows in rags watched the birds eat the seeds. Here and there a gnarled grape or rose vine made old-fashioned love to a faded porch. Most windows had wooden shutters, some of which probably shut. Some windows were wide open to a fluttering tatter of lace. Windows were smaller up near the top, suggesting that a child or a dwarf might live way up there by himself. All the roofs slanted, to let rain run off. Only the new antennas, shiny and straight, assured the passer-by that those inside were changing their channels.

Yet, right there on a lawn was an old codger as though tending his grapes. Some dadburned trouble with the blinking tube no doubt, he was waiting on his check before he had it fixed. If the blinking Legislature got off its bum, he'd have a nice new color in there and wouldn't be wasting his time messing about with these seedy old grapes. He wouldn't be out here subjecting his wrinkled old face to the potentially harmful rays of the sun, getting his poor cheeks all flushed by its warmth. He wouldn't be bent over like this feeling his white hair all fluttered by a dadburned breeze from the South. Wouldn't be risking a nasty nick from that knife, bother those busy doctor fellows at the clinic so soon again. Nick? Hell, a man could put out a blinking eye with a blade like that, if he didn't know how to handle it just right, which way to make his slice, how to carve a nice notch, flick out the white pulp, tap in. . . . What *was* this old man doing, grafting, his grapes? He scarcely glanced up as a stranger strode by. He gave a little nod, but did not say Wadyaknow or anything else. This character was absorbed in his work.

Well, there's one in every block. Any unemployed census taker-ice cream man-egg peddler knew that. The question was, how old was this man? What did they have on him down at the Department of Health, i.e. what was his life expectancy in years and months? If things looked good, if his card was half blank, that would be reason enough to go back to work. That man would be ready for an ice cream sandwich later on, at about five-thirty or six. An easygoing salesman could sell him a half-dozen eggs now and then if he wasn't all wrapped up in his cholesterol count. If he was still around in 1980, he would badly need a good census taker to cover up any self-incriminating little slips he might make. Such considerations as these made one think twice about remaining unemployed, or even hiding long in the trees. . . .

Phase Four glided by; the long short-wave aerials nodded at George. He was nearing home. No, ice cream would not be easy to sell in winter in Washington State. Nor did the hens lay well at this time of year. Better that he should pace himself. He waited for the aerials to nod out of sight, then quickened his step. He would reach home just after them, unless they had parked. Perhaps home would be deep in that fog, although he could not hear any horns. In any case Irene would have the radio on, in defiance of bugs. Fog or shine, radio or not, let them try to penetrate the code of her smile. Let them jam her laugh if they could. Meanwhile he would be telling her his thoughts about work. Then, if conditions were right, he had a few chores to do around the old house.

They weren't. Even from here he could see the bright sunshine drying the moss on the antennaless roof. On the bare ground out front, where the car should have been, the puddles of oil had dried scarcely at all. That southerly breeze toyed with the last leaf on the tree—just you wait. It fingered the dead grass on either side of the well-trodden path to the pump. The pump house itself, which some former tenant had painstakingly painted in Permanent Zinc, showed up well in this light. It glared at the plain grace of the weather-painted house. Clearly it sided with the shiny new telephone pole, to which it was linked by a taut, new length of wire. Its line to the house hung all tattered and slack. Out back, the breeze-rippled bay sparkled quite blindingly now, but not blindingly enough. From straight up in the sky it would still look like shit soup. Smiling he pushed open their front door, and Irene's answering smile shut everything out. All this smiling made for a rather lopsized kiss. "Hey there, ma'am," he said, his hand touching her beautiful neck.

"You look pleased," Irene said.

"I am."

Their kiss turned out all crooked again, and they backed

13

apart. She waved her fingers at him and turned the radio down. "Coffee?"

"Good," he said, for lately he had begun to enjoy drinking the stuff. One did not have to drink much when two shared a cup. As she went to the stove, he spotted mail on the table and sat down with it. Reaching for tobacco and papers on the window sill, he rolled a quick cigarette. "Hey, you must think you married some kind of hermit tycoon."

"Well, I was beginning to wonder," she said.

"Relax," he said, opening the telegram, "another year you'll be all flustered by the auto insurance bill. Well now . . ." Reading the first crazy words, he broke out in a laugh.

"What is it now?"

He finished reading and passed it along:

RECEIVED YOUR LETTER PLASS CALL BEFORS% AT 213985-4213 EXT 1911 COLLET OR AT MY HOME 975-966 AFTER 7 PM COLLECT AT YOUR CONVENIFCA BEST REGARDS
                                                BRENDON

"What will you do about that?" she asked.

"What will we do about this" he asked, passing her the next:

DEAR MR ALBERTS. I AM SPEAKING IN BEHALF OF WARMAN BROS. PICTURES AND AM NOT AN INDEPENDENT PRODUCER. IN OTHER WORDS, WE WOULD LIKE TO DEVELOPE A SCREENPLAY THAT WE WILL MAKE INTO A MOVIE, WITH A TOP-FLIGHT DIRECTOR. WE WOULD LIKE TO OFFER YOU THE INVITATION TO FLY DOWN TO HOLLYWOOD AT OUR EXPENSE, AND COME INTO WARMAN BROS., MEET WITH THE PEOPLE HERE AND DISCUSS THE PLANS WE HAVE FOR ADAPTING YOUR NOVEL INTO A MOTION PICTURE. WOULD YOU PLEASE HAVE YOUR AGENT OR YOURSELF CALL US COLLECT 545-6604 HOLLYWOOD, CALIFORNIA NEXT MONDAY. THE OTHER PERSON YOU ARE NEGOTIATING WITH IS PROBABLY AN INDEPENDENT PRODUCER WHO WOULD THEN HAVE TO TAKE THE NOVEL TO A MAJOR STUDIO PROBABLY US. THERE WOULD BE NO POINT IN YOUR HAVING TO GO THROUGH A MIDDLE MAN, WHEN YOU CAN DEAL WITH US DIRECTLY.
                        BILLY WILKINSON, WARMAN BROS.
                                                PICTURES
CC: JIM GREEN, PETER CROZIER, KARL HARMON

While she considered that he handed her the last:

THE NEW YEAR HAS PASSED AND I THOUGHT I WOULD START IT OFF BY ELLING YOU THAT AFTER MUCH DELIBERATION, WE THINK WE CAN WORK OUT A DEAL WHEREIN WE WOULD PURCHASE ONLY THE MOTION PICTURE RIGHTS IN AN OUTRIGHT MANNER SO THAT WE COULD FURTHER INSURE YOU THAT WE WOULD MAKE THE MOTION PICTURE. I AM AUTHORIZED TO OFFER YOU $20,000 AS THE PURCHASE PRICE FOR THE NOVEL IN ACCORDANCE WITH THE ABOVE MENTIONED TERMS. WILL YOU PLEASE CALL OR WIRE ME COLLECT AS SOON AS POSSIBLE. KINDEST REGARDS.
                              BILLY WILKINSON, WARMAN BROS.
                                                      PICTURES
CC: JIM GREEN, PETER CROZIER, KARL HARMON

Irene had worked in offices and banks. Sipping her coffee, she arranged the telegrams on the table in a row, comparing their dates. "They must have gotten your letter between that one and that one," she said, pointing.

"I guess," he said, rolling a cigarette.

"If you didn't use a post office box, you would have gotten all these last week."

"I suppose," he said. "Well, we had a nice week . . ."

"This one took five days," she said, holding one of the two-page ones up.

"Five days?"

"This one took four . . ."

"Which one is that?"

"The one about . . ."

They could bear it no longer. He started it, with a yelp of laughter that blew the paper out of her secretarially poised hand. Watching it go, she yelped too, and the paper fluttered upward, then settled down with the rest. Catching his breath, he pointed at that yellow bouquet. "I am speaking on behalf of . . ." he said. They looked across at one another, shaking in their chairs. "I am authorized to offer you . . ." They sat clasping their bellies in pain. They tipped forward, and there was a moment of silence after the hard crack of their heads. Then they were shrieking, pounding their foreheads separately on the table top, some distance apart. "I am offerized to author you . . ." He slipped off his chair onto the floor, lay writhing

15

there watching her slide off of hers. Out of the corners of his eyes he saw the cat slink into the hall. "How long did that middle one take?" he gasped between the table legs. "OWW-WEE," she wailed. "And that little one?" he called. "OWWO-WEE OWWOWEEEE," she begged, pounding her head on the floor. He was too weak to give her the coup de grâce. Flat on his back, straining for air, he watched a bug pass by the window, outside. Across from him, Irene lurched to a half-sitting position. "I am offerized . . . ," he called through the table legs, but it was too late.

"*Don't,*" Irene begged.

After some rest, he got to his feet. "Come finish your coffee," he said very levelly, gathering the telegrams up. Tucking them in their envelopes, he went to the cupboard and put them in the paper bag of this year's mail. He recurled the top of the bag and slammed the cupboard door shut. Back at the table, Irene was drinking her coffee in little gasps. He did not watch, but wandered about the room, discovering cobwebs never seen by man before.

"How was your morning?" she asked at last.

"Well, I . . ."

"The weather was clear," she helped.

"Yes!"

"You found the place all right?"

"Oh yes, it was easy."

"You took the bus?"

"Yes, on the way over . . ."

"And walked back?"

"Yes."

She turned the radio up. "There's something wrong with the Apocalypse," she said.

"I thought I heard something about that as I came in," he said.

"There's been no contact for an hour," Irene said. "They think they may have been hit by a meteor."

"No contact for an hour?"

"No."

He sat down to listen with her. There had been no contact for an hour, the man said.

"They're supposed to be about two hundred thousand miles from Mars," Irene said.

They should be less than two hundred thousand miles from Mars, the man said.

"Did they complete that rendezvous?"

"I don't know," Irene said.

Wall Street was down five points, the man said.

Irene said, "It's been a peculiar trip all along."

"Hasn't it?"

She turned the radio down. "Did you find out about the job?"

"No, the gate was locked."

"Ah, that's a shame."

"I got there about noon, maybe a few minutes after."

"What was it like?"

"Beautiful trees," he said. "Arbutus and evergreen. It looked like a good place to work."

"It sounds lovely." Through this window they could see their tree, the mud flats in the distance, no water at all now that the tide was out. "Well, it was a nice day for a walk," she said.

"Oh yes."

She stood up. "I suppose we should eat."

"I suppose we should."

"Does toasted cheese sandwiches sound all right?"

"Hm, just cheese perhaps."

"Cheese and bread?"

"Just cheese for me."

"I'll put out the bread. I think I'll have another cup of coffee too."

"I'll have milk," he said, going to the refrigerator.

She brought the bread and the cheese on separate plates. By way of compromise and companionship, he broke off half a slice of bread to go with his cheese. Munching dryly between gulps of their drinks, they gazed out at the day. "The water pressure is low again," she informed.

"I'll have to check the pump," he said, going to the sink and checking the tap instead. "There should be enough in the tank until evening, unless you're planning to wash. Don't flush too much."

"No," she said. "I was thinking this might be a nice afternoon to go to the beach."

"The beach?" He went to the rear window and looked out. "We could try it," he said.

"We can take the radio."

"Yes, and books." When he came back from the

livingroom with their library books, she was ready to go. It was one more thing he admired in her, she didn't have to put on a public guise every time she went out. In this case she had simply loosened her bright hair, taken off her shoes. She looked very young and carefree—*free*—and the buzz of a low-flying bug stung his heart. "Let's check the God damn pump on the way," he said, holding the door.

Outside, he studied the yard while she scowled at the sky. Why give them that satisfaction, he thought, and said to her: "Our leaf is still hanging on."

"Yes!"

In the pumphouse the pump chuckled dryly at them. "I'll prime it tonight," he said, yanking the plug. The pump rattled and died. He secured the shiny doorlatch with a good stick he had found to replace someone's galvanized spike. As they turned away, the breeze rattled the door softly. Smiling he followed Irene's halo down to the great, straight logs, helped her climb on. Someone else, earlier, had chosen these carefully, and anchored them well. In that man's memory a good tenant might well spend a few hours a week scrubbing the slime off them, although with both the tide and the sun out one could imagine Nature still in control of that. Even so Irene slowed down over the tidepools halfway across, as though they somehow offered a worse pitfall than the despoiled mud around. Wisely she slowed down whenever they had to step sidewise onto a new log. She jumped off the last one onto a board; he jumped twice as far onto seaweed and sprinted ahead.

Their beach was the spine of a sandspit, a few feet of dry sand where high tide rarely left jetsam and oil. They had it all to themselves. Often in summertime they had shared it with an old couple surrounded by windbreak, umbrella and other paraphernalia, sun lotion and beer, airedale and goose. "I wonder how they all are," Irene said spreading out, and he laughed. "Yes." Chin on hands he had a crab's-eye view of the scene, the shimmering water, the placid ships, the peacefully bustling docks. At this distance the muffled grating of machines seemed to hum in tune with the meaningless pings of their bells; the voices of the busy little men were lost somewhere in mid-air. Up there too, gulls silently circled forty-foot cranes,

18

perhaps waiting for them to drop a two-ton bite of canned tuna just in from Japan.

> Birds clutter
> the air
> That's fair

Down near the water, the little flags waved from the low-lying sterns, Japanese, British, U.S., Liberian, Argentinan, Japanese . . . Nearest by waved the Yugoslavian, the same that lately some student of the left or right had paused before their door to scrutinize, across the lap of his ladyfriend. It had turned out that he wished to scrutinize the shanty dwellers as well, and George had gone forth to give him a closer look. "I was just wondering where that ship's from." "I was wondering the same about those binoculars." After helping the man spell out the long, unpronounceable name of the ship, George had suggested he take one last look and drive on. "I'm sorry, sir!" the red-faced lady had pled, and George had smiled and waved her goodbye before turning away. Today that ship's cranes grated and pinged the same monotonous tune as the rest, just a little louder, from nearness. Ping ping, all chorused.

"Well, shall we buy one of those and cruise around the world?" he asked.

"Could we handle it alone?"

"Never."

"But you know about boats . . ."

"Ships." Probably she was recalling his telling her of the time when, at sixteen, he had helped steer the cruiseship *Borenquin* through "one of the worst storms of all time off the east coast of Florida"; no doubt she forgot his saying that the captain and the quartermaster had stood one on each side of him throughout. In fact all he had learned from that night was that he had a stronger stomach than most. In further fact, for someone who had spent two or three months of his life aboard ships, he found in himself a surprising ignorance of the sea. "Perhaps we should sign on as passengers," he said.

"Are sailors usually nice?"

"What? They can be. I knew an honest quartermaster once. Next to him I think the alcoholic drummer in the ship's band was best. I knew a black dishwasher on the *Aquitania* during the war, a middleweight prizefighter. I think he was in the Army though."

"Maybe we should get a little sailboat," she said.

"Can you sail?"

"Can't you?"

"Not much."

"Hm. Well, we could build a raft."

"Yes, right here," he said. "Out of this driftwood, these logs. Can you row?"

"I think so."

"Hm. Well, all we'd have to do would be paddle out a few miles. I think we could rely on the tides to carry us somewhere then."

"Where shall we go?"

"I'm not sure it will be our choice."

"You were a navigator, weren't you?"

"In the *air*. I could brush up on it easily enough, I guess. We'd need some kind of shelter to keep the charts dry, protect us from the sun and so on."

"How about the goose's umbrella?"

"Hm. Or a tree—an evergreen. We could cut a hole in the deck, put a box of good earth under there. We'd have to find some way to filter out the salt, of course."

"Or take plenty of fresh water to water it with."

"Maybe we'll have to settle for a tent instead. We could nail it right down to the deck."

"And load it with good food and books."

"Yes. And the radio?" The Apocalypse was still missing, the man said.

"Let's leave it behind." Irene turned it off.

"O.K. We can always get a cheap one in Japan if we change our minds. That's another thing—getting in and out of ports. What with all the inspections and licenses, it could take us a year to get off this spit."

"Maybe we could sneak out at night."

"Foggy night," he said. They looked out toward the open bay, where a big freighter was coming in, another going out. "How about going to Mexico?" he asked.

"By raft?"

"Car," he said.

"Miss Palsey of 1956?"

"We could try it. We could get another on the way south if she doesn't seem up to it. I could get another from the same man in Tucson. He's an honest man." He flipped a pebble into the water, saying, "Meanwhile I could give her a trial run to L.A."

"I gather you're not going to take them up on their plane ride."

"I had an offer like that from another would-be producer once, and lived to be thankful I'd paid my own way."

"You aren't going to take the twenty thousand dollars."

"Haven't I already turned down a hundred and twenty?"

"But that was for television rights."

"They'd still be offerized to awful it."

"You've decided on Brendon then."

"Probably."

"Are you going to call him?"

"Tonight."

She flipped her pebble, into the sand. "When are you leaving?"

"In a day or two," he said underbreath. A bug buzzed up behind them, and Irene turned the radio on. The man said there was still no sign of the Apocalypse. Houston was doing everything in its power though. Meanwhile that bug seemed to expect a splashdown in shit soup, if not on their very spit. Noting that Irene did not scowl up this time, George closed his eyes. "Wake me if they find anything," he said.

When had these docks been made, just a hundred years ago, when the Indians were still permitted to use their fishing nets? What had they thought when they saw those pilings being driven in? Had they known they would soon be swamped, or had they dreamt of riding the tide again? Had they sat in their boats scowling up, or looked down into the clear water in brooding thought? Whatever they had done, had not worked. "Buzz *off*," he said, and buzz off it did!

They lay on a while; around their spit the water looked tired, with the sun going down. One by one the little bells pinged off, the little lights blinked on, toting up the final score. One light for every hundred pings? The U.S. was doing very well, followed closely by Japan. Ah, here came England on—

21

perhaps their tabulating system had not yet been computerized. George waited for a little flurry from, he guessed, Liberia, and then sat up. "Let's go celebrate."

"Let's!"

"After all, we *have* been offerized."

"Yes!"

Now with soup crawling underneath, they crossed the logs quite cheerfully. They stopped at the house to exchange books and radio for shoes, and lock the door. "Have you change?" she asked, dropping the big key inside her purse.

"Some. We can get more at the grocery store."

"You'll need two or three dollars if you're not going to call collect."

"That's all right," he said. It was that hour of early dusk before car and street lights quite take hold, when visibility is least. It was the hour of the pedestrian, though few had yet discovered it. Most citizens sat in their houses behind closed Venetian blinds, or drove blindly home from work. Thus knowing strollers had sidewalks almost to themselves, hidden from driver, pilot, and resident alike. George gazed above the picture windows, the windshields, at the beautiful, invisible sky. "I wonder if there'll be a moon tonight."

Irene looked too. "I see a star."

"*Where?*"

"Just above that pole."

On closer study, she was right. At the corner a patrol car honked twice at them, pique, pique, for they had not shown up well enough. Smiling, hand in hand, they turned onto a darker street. Here the houses were packed in tight, the extra cars queued out front. These gleamed at pedestrians longingly, poor abandoned brutes, while the barking watchdogs watched. It was advisable to walk in the street, where the late returnees had to drive single-file, or honk and wait. Soon there would be no waiting room. Last one out of the parking lot is an astronaut: he'll end up orbiting his block all night. Oh, won't the bugs howl at that.

Irene said, "I wonder how they're doing up there."

"Ah yes, up there."

They stepped aside for an old man who desired their space. He waved after he'd made good use of it. "Wadaya know?"

"Good evening," they said, nodding at the fluorescent hat.

"I've seen him somewhere recently," Irene said underbreath when they were past.

"His cousins are everywhere."

Their store was just ahead, Rudy's Superette. It shed at this hour a baleful light, wreathing in oyster white the silent shoppers passing in and out. Were those edibles they trundled in last year's Safeway carts? At least these weren't the new-style litters manned by organized, sterilized ward boys on their grave way to surgery. At least Rudy's door was still propped open by two cartons of pineapple-grapefruit drink. At least his bargain signs were still writ by hand: Gruond Meat 3 # for 2.56 or 3.58. KLeenez 2 for double wiggle GIANT Size. "We'll have to be careful if you want telephone change," Irene warned between her teeth.

"Sherry then?"

"All right."

Passing the dour non-celebrants, they selected their sherry devil-may-care, not the medium sweet but the cocktail dry. Leading her to the other side of the store, he reached for anchovies—no, artichoke hearts. Up front, they selected six candy bars equally, three apiece. "Smile! You're on Candid Camera!" the cheerful sign at the checkstand read, and waiting he saw her scowl at the glowing red eyes above. He touched her purse.

"Oh yes, may we please have an extra dollar's worth of quarters?" she asked, finding her five-dollar bill.

Frowning, Rudy's wardenness plucked quarters out, tossed them on the stand to roll around. "Quarters on Number Two!" she barked into her mike, thus they left without saying thanks.

"You saw?" Irene asked outside. She sighed. "I guess we'll have to find a smaller store. They're getting smaller and smaller all the time. Well, that's the way it should be," she reminded herself. "People should support independent merchants instead of peeping finks."

He agreed, "As long as there are any left."

"There's that little Japanese store on Fourth, and that co-op on Twenty-first."

He laughed. "Anything is better than buying sherry from uniformed brats looking down on you from their

23

platforms like Ministers of Internal Affairs."

"Ah," she said, "I take it we'll not soon be returning to Canada."

"Not this trip. Hey think of the tiendas and mercados, open-aired. What time is it?"

"Ten minutes to."

"We can turn here and hit it about right," he said, but she had already turned. This was the Street of the Apartment House. Opposite lay a woods, and they naturally chose that side. At night, in wintertime, it was hard to say whether the trees were dead. The kleenez was blooming well on the blackberry vines. It was in season, of course. Today's breeze had helped waft the spores from the fertile refuse bins across the way. A good deep protective mulch lay everywhere. God knew what manner of little animals burrowed in there. They lived in a heady atmosphere, leavened now by traces of a hardy skunk. Marvelous to think how wildlife will persevere; that skunk had turned camoufleur.

Their telephone booth was faring not so well. All alone at night it glowed, forlorn, exposed, in a puddle of broken bottles and window glass. The door crunched open and they crunched in. "Did you bring your telegram?"

"They put the wrong number on it. I have the right one here." Together they stacked their change on the filthy stand. "Quarters on Number Two!" he barked, lifting the receiver up. Then he dialed one plus code plus everything.

"You can dial that number directly, sir."

"Didn't I?"

She did not dispute—he dialed again.

"Can I *help* you, sir?"

He bespoke his names and numbers hopefully.

"Will you be *paying* for this? One minute, sir . . . Deposit one-ninety when your party is on the line. One minute, sir."

He waited three.

"University Studios."

"This is Browns Point, Washington, operator. I have a call for Mr. Brendon O'Brien."

"One moment, Washington."

They waited two.

"Washington? Who's calling, please?"

24

"This is Browns Point, Washington, operator. I have . . ."

"*Brownspoint,* Washington!"

". . . Calling Mr. Brendon O'Brien . . ."

"Operator, this is University Studios. I have no Brendon O'Brien listed here."

"One moment, operator. *Sir?*"

"Brendon O'Brien. I believe he's acting in a movie there."

"This is a big studio, sir. I wouldn't know where to connect you, sir."

"Ah. Thank you, operators, I'll try again."

Collecting his change, he held the door while Irene squeezed crunching out. He stood beside her, inhaling night. "Well, that was cheap."

"We could have spent those quarters on food."

He relieved her of the grocery bag. Behind them lights flicked on, a motor started up. *Retenu.* "Hey we have our artichoke hearts!"

"Right now I'll settle for a hot cup of coffee."

"And a fire."

"Let's hope there's some water left."

The van cruised by, and shivering she took his arm and moved in close. "I wonder if there's any news."

"Ah ya, up there." The stars were out. "What did the weatherman have to say about tonight?"

"Clear and cold, I think."

"No fog?"

"I don't think he mentioned it."

"I thought I heard a horn . . ."

"So did I . . ."

"There it goes again," he said, and they hurried home on that happy note. Their key did work at once, though he had let another day go by without putting graphite in the lock. While Irene spooned coffee, he went to the sink and checked the tap. "Plenty! I'll prime the pump later," he called, going to the front porch for wood. They would be sitting in the livingroom tonight. In the light of the streetlamp, he quickly gathered an armload from the pile of extra fine and longest dried. Feeling its quality again, he remembered with a pang how much they had enjoyed collecting that from the cool wet sand, under a cloudless sky. Could human beings really adapt that well? A more comforting word was, *persevere.*

"You're using the good wood tonight," she observed.

"Yes—"

"I know: we've been *offerized.*"

"Yes!" One match, one sheet of newspaper started the Little Gorilla up. He slapped her shut and turned to warm his back, as Irene came in with coffee and cocktail dry. On a tray tonight, and the artichoke hearts on a dish. Her smile defied. He placed the little table in front of the sofa bed, and they sat around it cozily, the Little Gorilla, he, and she. Beside the dish lay the oyster fork.

She said, "We should have candlelight tonight."

"Yes." He was opening the sherry up.

"Shall I get it?"

"Have we some?"

"I think one stub."

"Oh, let's wait until the lights go out."

"Am I married to Washington Light & Power?"

"I'll get that stub."

On the way back he slapped off the switch, bore high the candle in its Cointreau holder. What had they been celebrating then? Ah yes, memory stabbed again: the Happers novel. When they accepted it? No, probably when they sent the check. No, that had been cognac with Miriam . . .

"Do you remember when we celebrated our first month's anniversary?"

"Yes!" With a flourish now, he set the candle in front of Irene's enchanted face. Enchanted, he touched glass to cup. "To Irene, my love."

"*Us.*"

The Little Gorilla was glowing red. It seemed to smile in the candlelight, as did the windows looking in from the seaward porch. The porch itself was dark—one could scarcely see the outer window panes. Not hard to imagine dense fog beyond, nor the total absorption of the dim shadows cast here within. The couch lay low and soft, its army blanket a rich upholstery. The candle's flame winked at the cocktail dry. He handed the glass to Irene. What a dainty sip she took to wash all that coffee down. He fed her an artichoke heart.

"Mmmm."

26

He tried one himself. "Fit for an astronaut."

"I wonder what could have happened up there."

"There must be almost infinite possibilities."

"Think of drifting away out there, completely out of touch with the Earth. How are they reacting to that?"

"Semi-automatically, I'd guess."

"They're still human beings."

"Partly—they've had a good deal trained out of them. They're busy fiddling with their dials. Maybe toward the end there would be an unprogrammed moment of human terror, when they thought of their families back in the world they left. They might ask themselves questions then. But probably they would be comforted by the thought of Christopher Columbus," he comfortingly said. On the other hand, Columbus got home—who remembers the names of all those hero skeletons they sailed above? "Right now it's Houston that's feeling sorry for itself. They've misplaced their tools."

"Still, you have to feel sorry . . ."

"I do!" he said. He went to the Little Gorilla, fed her a stick. Let's celebrate. "If you want to listen to the radio, Irene, go on."

She started up, sat back again.

"Go on. God knows what may be happening now."

He found himself straining to hear as she returned, but the man in Seattle had nothing new. He would keep-the-kiddies-up-on-the-latest-dope-from-Houston-though, just-as-soony-oony-o . . . Meanwhile-here-was-a-little-toony-oony-o-by-The-Public-Hair, Number 81-this-week. *I Want to Grab Your . . .*"

"Help!"

She did, and spun the dial while the machine was off. "Maybe we can get Jay Gardner."

"Try."

The soft voice was on edge tonight. ". . . Now let's see if we have that caller from Oakland on Line 4 . . . Jay Gardner speaking . . . He had something very interesting . . . *very startling* . . . Sir? Hello? . . . about a short-wave message he says he picked up, between Houston and . . . Let's let him tell you what he heard himself . . . Sir? Hello? Hello? . . . Paul? Folks, my producer has signalled me a station break. Hang on. We'll try to talk with that gentleman in a few minutes, said

27

he'd just intercepted a shortwave message out of Houston—it was a stunner folks. Hang on there. Back in a jiffy—God willing . . ."

The announcer came in to sell orange juice and horoscopes, remind everyone to register for free Social Security plates. After a pause, he mentioned orange juice again—rather desperately—and paused. Program music broke in, mid-note, too loud. The engineer turned it down almost as quickly as did Irene, and she turned it up again. Heads low over the radio, they listened to each languorous note. When the song coasted into another one, they turned to glance into each other's eyes. Where is he? In the men's room being beaten up? George touched her wrist and she held up her watch. One and a half minutes to. The song purred on until a rapid voice broke in to name the Jay Gardner show, the producer, the engineers. "Listen to the Jay Gardner show again tomorrow night. News next on KOO." After a pause, a deep, controlled voice announced no news of the Apocalypse. Irene switched off.

"To Jay Gardner," he said, and they drank in turn to that.

The candle was almost out. Irene snapped Washington Light & Power on again. Their vengeful bulb shone extra bright, wiping the smile off the Little Gorilla's sooty face. The windowpanes leered dirtily, reflecting the dirty blanket on the couch. George blew out the drowning candlelight. "Hey this is pretty good sherry," he said.

"Isn't it." She took a gulp, handed the glass to him. "I wonder if he got your letter," she said quietly.

"Mm." He went to the Gorilla and threw in a stick. "I'm quite sure he would have answered it," he murmured to the snapping flames.

"I'm not sure of anything," she said.

"I *trust* the man," he said to the slamming lid.

They sat in silence now beneath the glaring light. Let's celebrate. The Little Gorilla made a brave snap or two, but the sherry seemed to have lost its warmth. The tide was in, slapping the pilings beneath the house; now and then a floating log thumped the boards beneath their feet. "Probably I should start dinner," Irene said, standing up.

"I guess." Following her to the kitchen, he returned the Cointreau bottle to its shelf but left the sherry out. He thought

28

to finish reading his mail. He had already noted that his letter to the editors was not in the *Quarterly Bulletin,* and soon found why. They had needed that space to remind all League members that the Postal Service's deadline for mailing last Christmas's overseas parcels was November 28, domestic December 5. Well that they had! With 3,000 members, at say three parcels apiece, a veritable heap of mail might have plugged up the works for evermore. "Hey have you finished your mother's slippers yet?"

"Not quite."

"You'd better get to it!" Ah, there was further good news; this year members would be casting their election votes on computer cards. That way there would be no waiting half the night for those late returns to trickle in. Pouring sherry, he read on. "Photocop has taken over One Man Press," he announced, drinking up.

"Your letter wasn't in there," she said.

"No." He went to the door. If there was fog, it was not out front. Moonlight abetted the street lamp, the shed was coated with lunar caustic tonight. What, had they only been playing with those horns? Behind him he could hear that the water still held out, he could wait a while longer to prime. And Irene had the radio on, he would not want to miss the latest news. "Hey maybe it's a spacejacking," he said to her.

"Hm."

"Maybe they want to run the Man in the Moon for President?"

"Are you ready to eat?"

He went to eat. She had omitted the beans, he was pleased to see, and garnished the cheese with a ketchup sauce. There was bread. "Is that coffee I see in your cup?" he asked, pouring enough sherry for both of them.

"It's getting cold in here."

He went to the livingroom and fed the Gorilla three big hunks. Let's celebrate! On the way back he remembered to slap off Washington Light. Irene had remembered to turn off the radio. And to serve the salad with their main dish. One must eat if one would persevere. He would.

"I'm afraid that wasn't very much."

"It was quite enough."

29

"We can fill up on candy."

"Yes!" he said, lighting a cigarette. "I'll be right back."

In the bathroom he did not tax the resources of Washington Light, inadvertently flushed when he was through. Now it was time indeed to prime. The choking toilet sought to make water out of oxygen and hydrogen and random gasses, without success. In the kitchen Irene's eyebrows arched. "It's time!" he called, slipping out the door.

He hurried through the moon and star and lamp lit night, not to mention the picture windows and satellites. In the luminous shed he groped for the wrench among the tins. A former tenant had drunk his beer out here. "I better go prime the pump, Mom," with shaking head. "Don't be all night!" From the looks of things, Mom must have drawn pure brew out of her kitchen tap more than once. That would have brought Dad back. "L'il problem out there, Mom. Lemme test it first. Don't flush!" Hopefully George plugged in, poured water down the burping pump. She choked, and spewed it out. Ruefully he poured down another dose, which she swallowed with a shuddering gasp. Squatting well out of the way, hand ready on the outlet valve, he waited for her to drown or save herself. Seen through the door, the moon alone seemed to shine on the world below, on all the people sitting in their houses there, all the people lying there. What moons were shining on those four lost above? *Lost*. Beyond sight and sound and trace. Would anyone ever be able to say that again? The pump was chuckling now. He stood up, refilled her jugs. Her gauge said she would be all right tonight. Latching well her door, he started back down the old moonlit trail. There was a little sherry left, and candy, and time enough perhaps to celebrate.

TWO

With sunlight blazing through the bedspread-windowshade, he had used all eight corners of his pillow up, was ready to try Irene's. It would be cool by now, the underside at least. But the radio was blaring now, not just cajoling him. The spoon rang in the coffee cup. Smiling he sought his socks. They were close to hand, and his clothes were all together on the chair, denoting a formal evening. Ah yes. For all the blaze of light, the morning was a chilly one. He dressed quickly with a dive, a slide, a jump. On the way to the kitchen he tucked in his shirt. "Good morning!"

"Well, good morning!"

"What time is it?"

"Almost ten."

He stepped sidewise to bask between the warmth of smile and stove. "What's brand new?"

"Well, there's a rumor that someone has sent up a rescue ship."

"Ah."

"There's been no comment from Houston, but the President is going to speak tonight."

"At what time?"

"Seven our time—I think."

She handed him the coffee cup, and he did partake. "You've already been out?"

"We forgot milk last night. Your mail is on the table."

He stepped sidewise another step. "What, only one today!" He sat down and rolled a cigarette. Now opening the jaundiced envelope, he read:

RE "FXXE OXX" HAVING NOT HEARD FROM YOU RE-
GARDING "FXXE OXX" I MUST WITHDRAW OUR OFFER
UNTIL FURTHER NOTICE.
            —BILLY WILKINSON, WARMAN BROS. PICTURES
CC: JIM GREEN, PETER CROZIER, KARL HARMON

Irene was reading now. He handed her the cup; no, she
handed *him* the cup. They were laughing.

"We've been unofferized!"

"Stop!"

She leaned against him, he against her, and they sat
rocking there. It was too early for rolling, the floor was cold.
Soon their coffee began to slosh, and that sobered her. "Sit still
—your breakfast is almost ready," she sternly said, going to the
sink with the dripping cup.

He folded the telegram. Irene brought him coffee and
milk, presently an egg with toast.

"Eat it while it's warm," she said. Seated she read the
telegram off-handedly. "That one didn't take long to get here."

"No, it didn't."

"How long did they give you? Five days?"

"Five or six."

"I wonder if—"

"Not now," he grinning pled, and saw her reach rather
abashedly for the coffee cup. He asked gently, "How was your
walk?"

"It's a beautiful day."

"You found a store?"

"The Japanese one. It's on the way to the post office."

"That's right," he said. Half rising, he bent to kiss her
mouth. Coffee lipstick. He saw her flush, as though absolved.
He was absolved. "I'll have to go out soon myself," he said, but
sat down again and lit a cigarette.

"You're going to see about the car?"

"Yes."

"And take the papers to the school?"

"Yes, I guess."

She did not tell him it was late, but carried his dishes to
the sink. One thing she did not know was that today he
planned to arrive at the school a little late. Yet he bestirred
himself. He had kept the toilet waiting too long for its morning

32

flush. Wasn't the morning a bright one though. This window had a regular shade on it, which shed a pink light on the face he scraped. Adaptable, he allowed himself to be flattered by the fresh morning glow of it. But back in the kitchen Irene carried things a little too far. "You're beautiful," she said.

"In the light of your smile," he said. "All right if I wait to prime the pump when I get back?"

"Yes. Have you cigarettes?"

"Yes."

"And a check?"

"Yes."

"And the papers?"

"Ah yes," he said, going to the cupboard for the manilla envelope. As she came near, he tapped her backside with it. They managed an almost regular kiss, and once again at the door.

"Have fun."

"You too."

"Good luck."

"Never fear," he said, and kissed her once more before turning away.

Wasn't it lovely and bright. Last night's little man walked with his head tipped back, not to blind his sharp old eyes with the rays from his fluorescent hat. He did not interrogate today, not after last night's riposte. He relied mainly on his camera, no doubt. May your film be doubly blessed, old chap, if it has not already seen the light. Hey, you didn't miss that dog ahead? He does have a collar, yes, but did you check out the tag on it? Do the regulations permit a spaniel to wear his hair that long? The Department will want to add a shot of that to his file. Yes, little pal, the film's been hexed, but even so you might do well to sniff out another neighborhood. Attadog; he trotted off with a wagging tail.

Encouraged thus, a man could stride freely for a block or two, in a neighborhood lately snapped and sniffed. Wasn't it a lovely day. The air was fresh, the sun's rays were *new*. They had been sent forth in the same old way, to fall impartially on George, the street, a tree. Though the sun was low, it did not intrude. One did not see, but felt, its smile of amiable generosity. Thank you, old friend, George breathed. Ahead, a black cat darted across his path, furtively, the way they had used to do. It dove into the low branches of an evergreen shrub. Well done, my sweet. Good luck.

Twice comforted, a man could stride on and on, in brightest day. He made past Clinton's Electronic Auto Clinic and Repair, Inc., and now could discern the tarpaper roof of Bud's Garage ahead. At this distance the lofty totem pole out front appeared not an advertisement but some future dream, for which Bud's garage was tool house or workers' shed. Time would tell perhaps. Meanwhile a patrol car swung in. George slackened pace, remembering that he had thought to arrive at school a little late. Even at that he had to wait out the jolly cops, as he examined Miss Palsey, dismembered, upon the rack. It was a rear tire those others were worried about. They took turns kicking it each time the attendant gave it a little shot. One more should do her. There, that thumped just right. Waving they jumped into their car from left and right, made sure their motor had not stalled out. Eyes right they tooted thanks—lovely air you pump—and almost side-swiped a sober delivery truck. George turned to share the fun, but the grinning attendant was already hard at work on a nearby rack.

It was a day for tires. The attendant's job was first to take off the wheel. He did this by holding his big lug wrench far out at the end, where knuckles and sharp fender met. Down hard he pressed. "Ump!" he grunted, for that lug would not give, though the knuckles did. Blood gushed forth. "Ump! Ump!" The lug gave now, and blood coursed from the knuckle toward the wrist. Time to try another one. "Ump!" That was a start at least. "Ump! Ump!" There you go, all over the place. Fitting his wrench on another lug, the attendant paused, mustering strength and taking stock of goods on hand.

George shook his head. "Some way to start out the day."

The attendant grinned at him. "Oh, this is going to be a beautiful day!" he assured, and went ecstatically back to work.

Well yes, red did go well with his blue-glass eyes, his coal-black hair. George looked away. A Leghorn minced up to the Supermix pump. Peck, peck. Peck, peck. Was he trying to ring that bell? "Hey you've got a customer," George said.

The attendant glanced and scowled. "Belong to the lady in back," he said. "I'd shoot them in the head if I could get away with it."

34

George wandered over to Miss Palsey's rack. Behind him the attendant was working on a different wheel. Good God, he was rotating those tires. Ump! Ump! George wandered over, stood behind his back. Hey, you've got a customer. "Is Bud around?"

"Had to go to court."

"Ah. When do you expect him back?"

"Probably late."

George spun a wheel. "How long have you been working for him?"

Ump! "He's my father-in-law. I just got out of the Marines last week."

"Oh!" George thumped a tire. "Have any idea when this Chev will be ready?"

"What's the trouble with her?"

"That's what I hope to find out."

"Looks like her whole rear end is shot."

"It does at that."

"I wish I knew the bastard who invented an old-fashioned gizmo like that—I'd shoot him in the head."

"It might be a little late for blood." George spun one last wheel. "Tell Bud I'll try back again."

"Sure will."

"Take it easy."

The eyes rolled up, the grin beamed somewhere above George's head. "You know it, man," he said, and raised his dripping red hand in a half-salute.

"Ya." He was walking faster than was wonted now. Well, the robins too were too well seen in their naked trees. Against the sky each flick and flutter was clearly etched. Nonetheless, they still puffed their breasts, for a while more at least. The benign sun did shine on them, as on George, the street, the flag ahead. He slowed his pace. Was it the imagination or the sun that bathed the school itself in a harsher light? Wasn't the sun repelled too by the pale kiln-baked brick, so square and windowless? Did it really *want* to help all that synthetically stimulated grass to grow, encourage those lawns on which no one walked? It *seemed* to look upon them with a jaundiced eye, at any rate, which led to a discovery. Two acres of lawns, not one bird in sight.

George trod alone on the smooth cement out front. The flag's shadow flicked at his feet. Pale wads of chewing gum on the shallow steps were further signs of life. This school had entrances, eight of them, but he already knew that all but two were locked. You did have to push the heavy glass yourself. There was no decor in the soundproof mall, unless the isolated figures that glided by, and perhaps the doors. The first door stood to the left, where glowed the Administration Offices, opposite a board of photocopied bulletins. The book dispensary stood just beyond. In the very center lay a cement patio, where the sunlight took on a sallow cast through a dense glass roof which held off the sky. To the right, a grinning boy stood eyeing the door to the English cell, glass reflecting glass. George stepped around to show him how: one *pushed*. The grinning boy cared not one whit. Nor apparently that the bare-legged monitors were especially lush today, curled up on their little chairs like resting chorus girls. They fluttered their eyelashes, and George flicked back.

Through an open door an invisible teacher could be heard muttering English to her stupefied class. A mumbling man could be heard next door. But straight ahead an excited teacher talked to her attentive class. Her long auburn hair defied the artificial light, seemed almost to shine as though out-of-doors. Her head jerked sidewise as George approached, but then she smiled, as did her class, and George. Turning the corner he was pleased to hear her laugh. But now the English Office lay to the left, behind closed doors. He entered the first of these, caught a glimpse of catatonic faces in a further room within. Mr. White was addressing his class on tape today, with volume up: "The Schnook of Marysville thinks he's a Big Man. He thinks he knows as much as his teachers do. The Schnook thinks he can talk—"

The tape snapped off in mid-jeer, and Mr. White was muttering English to his silent class. Closeted with a student helper in scarcely space for one, George smiled at her as he slid past to deposit his manilla envelope in the tray. In the out-tray was a manilla envelope for Lay Reader Mrs. DeVoto, and a letter for Outside Reader Mr. Alberts—Personal. "Mr. Alberts, please stop by my classroom when you have a chance. Best wishes, Elizabeth Winthrop." He pocketed the note as he turned for help. "Can you tell me where I might find Miss Winthrop at this hour?"

"Miss Winthrop?" The blushing girl did wish to help. She turned to the photocopied schedule on the wall, and together they studied it. "It says she has her last Wednesday class at ten."

"Yes, that's what they said last week—but it proved not so."

"Well, Mr. White will be out in a minute or two."

"Thanks, I'll wait."

The signal sounded, the kids filed out the farther door. George and the helper stood straight. Glancing their way, Mr. White grimaced. Ah no, that turned out to be his smile as he drew near. "Wadaya know?"

"Hello!"

"Finding plenty of work?"

"There's only one batch today, for Mrs. DeVoto."

"Take it."

"Well . . ."

Reaching past George, Mr. White dipped a big hand into Mrs. DeVoto's tray. He had little curds of paper towel stuck all over his hastily shaven face, as though he moonlighted as Custodian of Marysville High. Where did he sleep, in the patio? "Oh yeah, that's the Uspensky book. Have you read it yet?"

"No."

"I'll get you a copy. The Special Classes will be working a lot with that." Mr. White returned to his classroom, knelt to the metal cabinet there, built like a safe. "You read the *Camillo?*" he asked, spinning dials.

"Yes, I've just returned some papers on that."

"Pretty good, eh?"

"Ya, that was a tricky one. I was happy to see that some of the students saw through it though."

"Oh?" Mr. White rummaged among his Comp Lit books and questionnaires. "I don't seem to have a copy of the Uspensky play—my other Lay Readers must have them all. The *Camp* comes later. I can give you a copy of the *Manifesto.*"

"That's all right. I'll be out of town a few days anyway."

"Good." Mr. White relocked his safe.

37

"Have you any idea where Miss Winthrop can be found?" George asked.

Mr. White strode to his schedule. "This is her early morning. Her first class was at six, her last was at ten."

"We tried that last week, but it didn't work."

"Have you tried the teachers' lounge?"

"Not today."

"Let's take a look."

"Fine!"

A smile flashed on the helper's face as George followed out. The halls were clear, except for one formidable lady standing guard, in case. Here came an invader now, all abashed and pimple-faced. "You know no one is allowed in this wing during lunch!" "I forgot my books." "*Fast.*" That left the halls quite bare. The monitors' chairs looked nude. The last traces of perfume were succumbing to the disinfected air. Mr. White opened the Private door.

All heads jerked up. A nearby teacher slid a smile past Mr. White, at George; that man had refused to shake hands two weeks before. Ignoring the man, Mr. White strode on to where the ladies sat. He pulled up a chair and sprawled on it, showing them a smile full of paper curds. "Sit down, Mr. Alberts. Ladies, you know Mr. Alberts, one of our new Lay Readers."

"Oh, Mr. Alberts!"

"Mr. Alberts!"

"It's nice to meet you, Mr. Alberts."

Bowing, Mr. Alberts sat down.

Mr. White raised a sardonic curd. "Liz, he's the man that was looking for you."

"Yes, I was looking for *him!*" She had a clear, self-assured face. Of the four, she was one of two or three who looked real.

"I'm sorry to be so slow in answering your notes," George said. "I seem always to have been here at the wrong time."

Miss Winthrop put down her coffee cup. "I just wanted to tell you how much I appreciate the beautiful work you do with my papers. I love your comments, and your attention to content as well as mechanics. And your 'people *who*'—"

"Hey, you're embarrassing the poor man—" Mr. White put in.

38

"Let her go on—she's doing fine!"

Miss Winthrop smiled over her cup. "I'll have a big batch of papers for you on Friday. You got those we did last week?"

"Which ones were those?"

"On *Gatsby?*"

"No, I'm sorry I didn't."

"We're going to have to stop choosing particular Lay Readers," Mr. White said. "It screws up the works. It'll be first come, first served. Anyhow, Mr. Alberts is going out of town for a while."

"Yes, for a few days."

"I'll hold them until Monday then," Miss Winthrop said. "My students have been begging for extra time anyway."

"Hey, you left the party early last night, didn't you, Liz."

"Yes, I had a cold."

"I didn't stay long myself, just a beer or two. I'm usually good for half a dozen, but I thought it tasted a little bitter last night."

Miss Winthrop and two others stared at Mr. White, while he winked at the fourth. "I thought so too," Miss Winthrop said, putting her coffee down.

Mr. White heaved to his feet. "Well, take care of that cold . . ."

"I will!"

Taking George in hand, Mr. White marched out of there. George answered little waves behind his back, and softly closed the Private door. Mr. White shot him a vicious glance. "I'll have something for you on Monday," he clearly hissed.

"Good, I'll see you then!" Waving, heading for the mall, George braced himself. The grinning boy was gone, but not the female guard. The blow struck his legs as he pushed the door. A heavy mace it was today, but he gave no outward sign, he felt. *Persevere.* He made it to the Administration Offices without breaking stride.

The air was clearer in here; perhaps they piped it in from a few acres off, filtered it through wet paper towels. Straight ahead two pretty girls sat typing in this room within a room, softly lighted, carpeted, a transparent front to the one-way glass that served as walls. No doors were readily visible, but George turned into the Secretary's cache, he knew just where.

Ms. Warner turned from her machine with glassy eyes. George waved and smiled.

"Excuse me," she said to her machine, and "*Yes?*" to George.

"I just wanted to leave my hours," he said, "and—"

"Leave them on the desk."

While Ms. Warner attended her machine, George did as he was told. She was punching buttons, now, reading from a card she held, and the machine did not seem to understand. It blinked in red alarm. Ms. Warner flipped a switch. Now a single yellow light blinked urgently, far up in the righthand corner of the machine, patently beyond her ken. It seemed to hold a clue. Perhaps Ms. Warner was too short for her machine? George thought to be of help, but something about the tense, hunched back said no. He blew his nose instead. "*Yes?*" Ms. Warner swung around, and the machine looked flabbergasted now.

"I wanted to ask you if you could mail my check this time."

"Have I your address?"

"I don't know." He had filled out his application, signed the loyalty oath, at City Hall.

Ms. Warner groped for a pad, found none. "Write it on your hours."

George wrote carefully beneath his hours. Ms. Warner and her machine faced one another in real panic now. "Thanks!" George called, and waved. Ta ta, Rob. May your wires live everlastingly in the Sign of the Cross.

Back through glass, past hard-typing girls, he pushed his way to the mall, and out. Five minutes in the decompression chamber had restored his legs to strong. He took the cement stairs by two's and three's, strode past Old Glory's bedraggled shadow on the walk. Warm sunlight welcomed him across the street, and he slowed in that. A clear voice said, "Hi!" "Hi there!" George said, and they exchanged smiles over the nodding head of a hobbyhorse. Is your mother as friendly, dear? What do you make of Big Bro and Sis these days? You're lucky to have the world to yourself for at least half a day, until they come home to show you what they've learned in the factory. Ahead, a tiny one hopped neatly on a sidewalk bedaubed with SHIT. A big five-year-old tossed pebbles at SNIFF IS GOOD on a garage wall beyond. These houses were all the same of course, so close to the factory, their markings alone served to distinguish them: I live next to the yellow SNIFF, ten squares past SHIT. Drop in sometime.

Thanks. George veered off to an older neighborhood. Here, where houses were farther apart, children had their world to themselves all day, Big Bro and Sis went to an old-fashioned school. This was an ice cream man's paradise. Did he only imagine that his audience looked up expectantly? Disappointed they must have been, but one sent him the same clear "Hi!" George replied in the same way too, smiling perhaps a bit more openly. His friend seemed satisfied.

He turned into a handy Circle C. The lone man in there was a substitute or new, he did not have the circled, appraising eyes. In fact he smiled and called out "Hi!" George replied in kind. He did not have much to buy; Irene would not have wasted a visit to a neighborly store, but he selected a box of Wheat Thins, always safe. Behind his back the hastily summoned cars could be heard converging on the parking lot, and already the intense shoppers were jostling him. Sidling past a big mother perusing non-animal milk, George chose three Lucky beers. By now the man behind the counter had lost the best part of his smile, however hard he tried. His staring customers queued up as he tapped on his adding machine, yet he paused to look George in the eye. "Will there be anything else, sir?"

"Have you an extra dollar's worth of quarters?"

"Certainly, sir." New or not, he traded monies in almost the same motion with which he sacked groceries, and with an untrembling hand. "Thank you, sir."

"Thank you!"

The man lifted the sack across the counter to George. Was that, "Good luck to you, sir!"?

"Thanks!"

He had to sidle carefully among the little cars outside, Lucky sack held high. Telling Mr. White of his travel plans had been a slip, perhaps. Yet it gave the radio patrol some exercise, and put them onto a seeming trail. Good strategy involved doing at least two things at once, one of them obvious. Thus he

41

zigzagged for several blocks, he himself knew not where until he sighted an empty booth and zagged toward that. It was an elderly one, not yet condemned. Recent tenants had left during the night, it looked, after a farewell bust. Young adults, he guessed. An unfamilial garbage littered the yard, a beer can propped open the door. That did help the air inside. Ah, they had taken the library along with them. No matter, he had brought his own, and it pleased him that they were literate. Could not only read, but write. For a good fix phone Marianne 364-0309. He dialed one plus code instead.

"Can I help you, sir?"

"Yes—"

"Deposit $1.10 when your party answers, sir."

"Thanks . . ."

"Jay Gardner's."

"Jay Gardner?"

"Just a minute."

"Thanks . . ."

"Hello?"

"Jay Gardner?"

"Yes."

"This is the Jay Gardner of KOO?"

"No, this is Jay Gardner's Tire Shop."

"Oh."

"A number of people have called looking for him. The name's just a coincidence. He's no relation of mine."

"You don't by chance know where he can be reached?"

"No, I'm sorry, I have no idea."

"Well, thank you. Sorry to have bothered you."

"Not at all."

"Goodbye."

"Goodbye."

George withdrew from the unlucky shack. At least the man had had a clear and friendly voice—one knew where to buy tires in California. He continued on straight ahead this time. Elm Street led to another booth, beneath a lovely Oak. He had spotted it one day when he was lost. New in town, he had thought to settle in this neighborhood, but its residents knew when they were well off. Not one room on Elm for rent, not even the oak's treehouse. Ten or twelve boys had that. It was just as well, for a few days later he had found Irene in her dreamhouse on the bay. He liked to walk down Elm Street for from time to time; it pleased him never to see a house for rent. He had not yet tried this booth.

This one had a book. He only used it in case they had changed the numbers since last week. They had not, but he dialed quickly, to be safe.

"Hey hey heyaway. Yes?"

"I wonder if you have a car for Los Angeles?"

"Los Angeles. What's your name?"

"Alberts."

"First name?"

"George."

"O.K., George. Call me tomorrow morning around ten."

"Thanks!" He dialed again.

"Hello."

"Hello. I wonder if you have a car going to the Los Angeles area tomorrow."

"I've got a '66 Valva for Downey—that's about thirty miles south of L.A.—you know the area?"

"Oh yes. Will that be ready to go in the morning, do you think?"

"Sure will. It's been sitting here for a week."

"Ah, you'll save it for me then?"

"Sure will."

"In the morning then."

"In the morning."

Now he was on his way, though it might not have looked so to the passerby. George strolled, enjoying Elm. A wind had risen, bringing cloud, besides. Children looked at him less hopefully, mothers called from half-opened doors. Was it the wind alone that prompted them, or had they too recognized the bleak eye of a cameraman driving by. They were not calling in the next street George chose, where children were at play in an equal wind.

George turned another corner, onto a street of pre-fabricated factories. A change of pace went unnoticed here, where workers spilled out of sheds onto parking lots, having just now punched the clock. They ran all stiff-legged to their cars, for they had spent six and a half hours making tote goats for their brothers in Detroit. Once behind the wheel, they loosened up. Now began the fun: Last one out of the parking lot . . . Cruncch, there came a little fender-dent, and two hopped out to look. Never mind, no need to call the pigs. The wife has another at home. Time to junk this one anyhow, give a little over-time to our brothers in Detroit. Hey dig that uncle on his feet—he must *really* have piled his heap. Passing several hundred of them at the light, George strolled home from work.

Their house lay under a lovely cloud, fat and wet, loaded with atmosphere. Yet loathe to precipitate. What had he read? The Northwest was suffering a serious shortage of silver nitrate and airborne dust, noted by the Department of the Interior? Sen. Mercy was looking into it; there was some question in his mind whether the shortage was contrived or not. Meanwhile swing low, sweet cloud, squeeze hard, don't let's wait for the committee to file its report. Meanwhile too the rapt house lay half in sun and half in the six o'clock shadow of Daylight Saving Time, its windows and door flung open wide. Irene was airing the listless bugs no doubt, the little creatures would be pining in the walls for news of him. Now he could hear her pure voice raised in song to them, and detect the heady aroma of oregano. "Hello, is anyone home?" he called.

Turning from the stove, she laughed in High C, or D perhaps, he would never know. "George! I was afraid you had already left."

"You know I wouldn't do that," he said, open-armed.

"Hug me, hugme, hugme," she pled. "How was I to know?"

"You know me well, Miss Mighty Hug."

"I imagined hearing from you in Oregon."

"Without a telephone?"

"You might have sent a telegram."

Not one in sight. Let's celebrate! "Is that a cool beer I see over there?"

"Yes, sit down!" She had started for the refrigerator, but leapt spread-eagle on his lap instead. "Mm, kiss me, kissme, kissme. Ah, I'm sorry—you wanted . . ."

"We'll share yours," he said, kissing her first. One lukewarm swallow was his share.

"I'll get another! You know, I had a lovely experience at

44

the store today. There was this lady, rather old, with a very good face, no makeup at all, very well dressed. She was asking another lady how to get someplace, but the other lady was new here too. When I told her which way to go, she said she was from Vancouver but had never been here before. She had always wanted to see Point Defiance Park, and finally some business had brought her here. Then it turned out the other lady was from Vancouver too, and I told her how to get where *she* wanted to go. We all parted friends, and they started off together on their separate ways."

When she paused, "Yes, that's nice," he said.

"You know, the old lady had a really exquisite diamond on her finger, no other jewelry or makeup of any kind. It made me sense how she must imagine her life somehow *hangs* on that."

"Hm. Yes, I suppose that's her talisman."

Irene shared a quiet moment with such a lady. "You're *my* talisman," she said, patting his head.

"What, are you polishing it?"

She laughed and kissed. "What's *your* news? Did you get the car?"

"No, Bud is in court today. Meanwhile the Marines have captured it."

"Will it be ready soon?"

"They couldn't say." Nor could he, quite yet, that he would be leaving in the morning by Driveaway.

"Did you find Mr. White?"

"Yes, with little curds of paper all over his chin. I think he's camping in the school these nights. Do you suppose he uses those themes for paper towels?"

"He probably wipes his ass with yours."

"Nevermore."

She was riding his lap again, smiling on him while he tilted their beer. "You're beautiful."

"Yes, you are," he said, returning her smile, watching it flow out in pink waves from her lips. "Your entire body is smiling."

"Yes, it's in love."

He kissed the smiling tip of her chin, watched her little hand take the bottle up. "You've noticed our cloud?"

45

Patting his shoulder with one smiling hand, tilting beer with the other, she nodded and drank simultaneously, one eyebrow arched toward the window. "I wish it would fucking well do something."

He laughed. "That's all right," he said, retrieving his half of the beer. "We'll find a way to seed it soon."

"How?" She watched his eyes wander over her radiant body. "I'll go get ready!"

"Hm," he said, frowning, sniffing. "Didn't I smell dinner cooking?"

"Hm," she said, and her frowning body leapt from his lap to the stove. "Damn! I don't know why I always burn the rice!"

"You don't always burn the rice. In fact I don't remember your ever doing it before."

"I remember another time."

He laughed. "You have a warped sense of always, ma'am. Twice is more like coincidence."

"George, can't you shut up while I'm burning dinner!"

"Always," he assured.

Having assigned half the rice to heaven, half to hell, she was all smile again. "I made a nice sauce I hope you'll like."

"I can smell I will."

"Are you ready to eat?"

"First can we finish our beer?"

"Of course," she said, helping him. "We're having salad too. Can you guess?"

"Ah, Cleopatra's Salad?"

"Yes!"

"Marvelous!" he said kissing her twice, peering into the refrigerator. Tonight she had chosen not one but two of her specialties. He could not keep in mind her exotic names for most of the traditional ones, others she created spontaneously, thus he had his own nomenclature for all. Tonight it was Cleopatra's Salad and, she would have been surprised to know, Rice with Mushroom and Olive Parmesan Vegetal. In short, she was going for broke.

She began heaping his plate with Vegetal. "We had quite a few odds and ends of vegetables."

"I see we did."

"There, that's enough to start. We can always have

46

seconds," she said. Quickly she pushed aside bottles and bowls, papers and books, clearing table space. Seated at the corner knees to knees, face to face, they ate in silent enjoyment for a while; but he could not long withstand her pleased yet beseeching eyes.

"Mmhmmm, the answer is: Beautiful."

"It is good, isn't it. I was afraid the mushrooms might be overwhelmed by the olives and celery."

"Not at all. Everything goes together perfectly. And to think all I smelled at first was oregano."

"Do you think there's too much oregano?"

"No no, that was outside," he assured. "Did I hear you teaching the little fellows some Hebrew songs tonight?"

"The what . . . ? Oh yes, it's time they learned their prayers."

They ate in silence for awhile, letting the little fellows meditate. Soon Irene put down her fork; George did too; click, clik. Bug that.

"I'm full," she said.

"I too."

"Well, we can finish it . . . Ah, I'll be eating it all alone, won't I, George?"

He nodded yes. "I have a driveaway for L.A."

"When?"

"In the morning."

"Shall we have our salad later?"

"Let's."

Up on her feet she was all asmile again. "I'll go get ready then."

"Good, I'll be finishing the beer."

"Bring it into the bedroom with you!" she called from the hall.

Laughing he followed her. Removing books from their bedtable, he cleared a little space beside his ashtray for cigarettes, tobacco, beer. Hard to say whether she had prepared the bed for him, or not made it yet. Seated on the edge of it, he had time to remove his shoes and socks before she came running barefoot down the hall; she reserved her efficiency for the important things. As she burst into the bedroom, he opportunely dropped his pants.

47

"*Well*," she said, not by way of criticism or reproof.

"Ma'am, aren't you going to pull up your dress?"

"Sir, what for?"

He waved reply. Smiling pink, she pulled her dress up and off. She had left her panties somewhere along the way. "Well?"

"*Well*," he said.

She laughed a high note, leapt past him into bed. From beneath a blanket the awakened cat blinked at each of them. Yawning, stretching, she plumped off the bed, made for the door rather doggedly. They had to laugh. *She* knew when it was time to eat. They could hear her loudly at it in the hall.

"We love you, Patter!"

"Don't go away mad!"

Crunch. Crunch.

Laughing he jumped into bed, snuggled up to Irene for warmth, at first. Seductive warmth, it led to a soft intermingling of thighs, and smiles. Are you gentle, sir? Oh yes. But not too gentle? Oh no! In unbecoming modesty she had left her brassiere for him to work off, but he gave preliminary attention to more accessible points, a tiny ear, a plump pink shoulder, a soft patch of neck, loose, smiling lips. Soon the rolling of her hips lured his hands astray.

"Oo!"

"Are my hands cold?"

"A little, yes."

"Pardon me, ma'am, so is your butt," he said, warming them there by way of compromise.

Now he could feel her little hands play lightly over his belly and hips, and her smile took on something like wonderment. "If you're so old, how come you're so soft?" she asked.

"Me? I'm just a growing boy."

"Yet you're so hard underneath. You haven't an ounce of extra weight on you, while I roll in it."

"Roll on," he said, pricking the crack in her writhing mound. A perfect sheath. Astraddle now, he let his warmed hands slide up her back while she reached out to his rapier, examining it with an almost unbearable gentleness. "Careful— that's a dangerous weapon in the hands of little girls." Smiling widely at him, she played deftly with balls. Clearly there was

48

no time for just hanging around. One, two, three, hooks and eyes were well-behaved tonight; he quickly slipped off her bra, let it fly with his shirt. "Ah, what have we here, little girl? Who could have guessed you had so much to hide?" Gathering a breast in each hand, he kissed their rosey nipples by turns, watching them swell beneath his eyes. "Shall I squeeze them?"

"Yes!"

Squeezing he asked, "Hard?"

"Yes!"

He squeezed until the smile left her lips and they were curling, writhing, sucking, all at once, as though hungry for pain. "What now, little girl?"

"Anything!"

He reached down to her gaping hole which writhed and sucked against his thigh, as though ready to take that inside. Gently his fingertips traced the wide-spread rim, around, around, then firmly seized and brought it closed. "Do you want more?"

"I want you inside me!"

Rearing back, he took aim. For all her tossing, rapier and sheath were in concert tonight, he pierced her on first quick thrust. At her "Ahhh!" he sat back, watched her climbing his lap, burying his rapier deep inside her, to the hilt. Then, leaning forward, pressing her breasts together, face to face, he withdrew himself, all but the tip. "What do you want now?" he asked.

"I want you all the way inside me!"

"Want what inside?"

"Your cock!"

"Ma'am, you mean you're ready to fuck?"

"Yes," she breathed, so he eased himself down on her, kissing each flaming breast before flattening both, kissing her widespread lips as he went by. In order to extend his rapier all the way inside of her, he had to press his chest against her averted face, thus she was left mouthing oo's and ah's to bony ribs. He had taught her early not to bite. Now it was easy to catch the insides of her knees in the crooks of his arms, fold them high above her golden head until he had her wild-haired mound exposed to direct attack. By sliding one willing knee onto his shoulder, he could reach a hand down to probe the

49

plump rear end in search of another, less overt hole. That tautness went slack as soon as he penetrated it, his finger slid on in until it came upon the larger tool hard at work on the other side of a smooth and pliant wall. Halloo, dark in here, isn't it? Yes, but nice! The poor little fellow would never, never know how nice. Yet he gave good account of himself as they joined in dance.

"Are we doing it now?"

"Yes. Oh yeees . . ." Irene was content to be led by him, she went almost limp, rocking gently under his rolling hips. Her eyes were closed, but not her mouth. When soon he began rearing back, thrusting deep, he could feel her slobber on his chest with each moan and yelp.

"And now?"

Her answer was a moaning yelp, while her legs broke free and locked themselves around his bucking butt. Now when he reared back she clung to him, their bodies were glued together in a churning dance, nailed at the crotch. Inside, it was up to his overwrought rapier to wield itself, thrash wildly from side to side, goaded by an excited fingertip. In the heat of struggle all parts are on their own yet joined in an unwitting conspiracy: together they bring two opposing bodies one shared victory. In the sudden gush of it, he gasped while Irene howled out her relief in what seemed a mixture of awe and agony. Gasping now for breath, rocking slowly back to earth in the soft cradle of her self, he watched her cry become a smile that he took for both congratulation and pride.

"Omnnn . . ."

"Unh?"

"Omumnum . . ."

"Mmm . . ."

"That was nice."

"Mmmmm," he said. They were both asleep, though he could sense he had not turned out the light. At best he could not have found the strength or heart to break from her slack embrace. Feeling himself crushing her ever more heavily with his sleep, he sought to levitate. She sighed, in thanks? He sighed back. When finally she did free herself by patting his thigh, stroking his hip, he simply hung there and let her float out. Omumnumuno, sweet love. Omunumuno, bright light . . .

50

Sometime later, hours according to the ho-humming clock, he awoke to find Irene still limp, one hand flung out upon his rump, her face averted from the glaring lamp. It was time he made use of those accumulated watts. Sliding smoothly toward the bed table, he felt little fingers flutter wistful pleas along his leg, but he did not stop, for he was overdue for a postprandial cigarette. Ah, and it was worth waiting for; all those lumens had not been wasted after all, they had been busy ripening his Half and Half to heavenly. They had also ripened up his beer, and raised its temperature, not bad fare at all on a winter's night. Behind him Irene bestirred herself and kissed his neck.

"I love you."

"I love you. Do you want some beer?"

"Ugh," she said.

"You want to sleep some more?"

"I don't know," she said. "Are you ready for salad yet?"

"Hm, not quite."

"Then maybe I will sleep a little more."

"Jay Gardner will be on soon."

"Then let's get up."

"Agreed," he said, retrieving her bra, his shirt. On his way out the door, he passed the cat. "Hello there, Patter!"

"Welcome back!"

On the way to the bathroom was evidence she had had herself quite a time. She had pitched half her chows into her water bowl, a kind of golf. She would return in a little while, to fish. He himself had sunk three or four in a row before looking around to find that he had backed carelessly into a trap. "Irene, is there any toilet paper in the house?"

"Oh, sorry!"

Resplendent in panties and bra, she proffered a roll to him enthroned. Now she waited to see how his majesty made use of it, or was she awaiting permission to leave? No matter, modesty is a plebeian trait.

"You *fold* it, don't you?"

"Oh yes."

"I just tear a handful off."

"Think of all those trees you waste.

"Oh, I always buy recycled," she explained.

"Recycle that," he said, and flushed the bowl. But after

51

washing his hands, he cupped her chin and kissed her on the forehead lightly on his passage to the hall. *Lèse majesté* overlooked.

Out front it was clear the Ways and Means Committee had not acted favorably on the Mercy report, a swarm of lights twinkled impishly from across the bay, while midway a sleepless tugboat glared at him fixedly. Avast, Cyclops, sleep. Cyclops did not blink. What were those lights above, the Goodyear blimp trying to nudge their cloud away? Hang in, staunch cloud, we're working on that silver nitrate, meanwhile your H_2O is many times heavier than He. From the kitchen Irene quietly added her prayers to that. "Did you mean me too?" he called. "Is it time I learned my prayers?"

"You! Only if you want to, George."

"It's doubtful I ever will, you know. In school I used to just mouth 'The Star Spangled Banner,' not to appear to subvert the State."

"Exactly! For God's sake, stick with 'Joshua Fit the Battle of Jericho,' *please.*"

"Can we make that 'The-Thigh-Bone-Is-Connected-to-the-Hip-Bone'?"

"That is a great song, isn't it?" She hugged him firmly from the back. "*See,* we always manage to compromise, somehow, don't we?"

"Yes." He turned to join the hug.

"Are you ready for salad now?"

"First shall we have a beer?"

"Oh, I guess so," she said, and went to the kitchen with him hand-in-hand. Seated at the table knees-to-knees, they had to smile as they drank his beer. She took a sip or two by way of conviviality. She did not smoke cigarettes, which made life cheaper and simpler for them, but confusing too whenever he passed his to Miriam. Would he never get over that?

"Do you think she minds?"

"Ma'am?"

"Being fixed?"

"Ah, Patter." The cat was spread out on her back before the stove, undulant, her manner both fretful and sensuous. "I myself wouldn't have the heart to wish it on anyone," he reluctantly said, adding quickly "but I think they may have missed."

"You really think so?"

"Look at her."

They did, and peering back at them through half-closed eyes Patter turned exhibitionist.

"Why doesn't she have babies then?"

"For one good reason, she never goes out."

"But wouldn't she go out, I mean otherwise?"

"Maybe she's been hypnotized. That's it, they gave her some kind of simple fresh-airophobia and charged you for surgery."

"George, you're making fun of my Patty-Pet—or of me?"

The cat stood up, arched her back, glided out of there. "There she goes," George said. "I broke the spell. You can look for some fluffy little ones in six weeks' time."

"No thanks—I'll settle for one little bald one of my own. Oh, I can't wait, can you!"

"Well, a while."

"Let's not wait too long, old man," she smiling said, gently stroking the top of his head.

He laughed and turned on the radio. "Don't worry about that, ma'am," he said, and called: "Patter, she's making fun of me!"

The man announced that in the absence of Jay Gardner they would have an evening of Frisco's favorite friskies. Like "Slap My Mother-lovin' Face with a Soft Balloon."

"Shall we have our salad now?"

"Let's."

They left the radio at half-hearted, just in case. He fetched the chick peas from the topmost shelf, the rice wine vinegar from the next, while she drew a bowl from the cupboard underneath. Unsure what other ingredients she would use tonight, he retreated to the table with his beer, to wait. Seeing her struggle with the catsup cap, he hurried over to unscrew that. Wiping her hands on the dish towel, she indicated the vinegar bottle too. Next she asked if he would mind getting the artichoke hearts and opening them, while he was up. Not at all! He took a luscious forkful as recompense. Back at the table, he watched her set to work. "Do you often make this salad when you're alone, Irene?"

"When would I have had the chance? I made it up just for you, that first night you came to dinner."

"I remember well."

Smiling they kissed to that memory, trading nectar of artichoke heart. The remainder she poured into her salad bowl. Now her prestigious hands danced among ther three shelves of spices, plucking and pouring almost faster than the entranced eye could watch. Each can and bottle flew back to its allotted niche in the rack, the entire kitchen hung suspended in an ambrosial cloud. Record that, little fellows. Goodyear, blimp that aside. They savored Cleopatra's Salad in speechless harmony.

Yet they could not quite finish it. Irene sighed. "We can have seconds later."

"Yes."

"Do you remember, we couldn't finish it that first night either?" She covered the bowl with a dish, and put it in the refrigerator, as she had then. "I invited you back for dinner the next night."

"And I offered to bring anchovies."

Irene smiled but did not laugh at him.

"When you said no, I believe I brought you a bag of traif orange slices instead."

She smiled again. "You didn't know gelatin was made of hoofs."

"In fact, I hadn't even realized you were a vegetarian."

"You still don't seem to realize that vegetarianism has nothing to do with traif."

"Sorry," he apologized.

"Excused."

"Then would it be traif if I were to invite you to bed twice tonight?"

Snuggling she said, "What, only twice? I remember the first night."

"That was the second night," he corrected her. "The first night I went home like some sort of gentleman. Were you impressed?"

"Oh, very much," she said. "Or was that disappointment that I felt?"

"I'd promised. I gained your trust. I showed you I wasn't just some old bum. And we've had plenty of time to make up for that first night, as it's turned out. Shall we now?"

Kissing him she asked, "Shall we wait for a little while?"

"We can have seconds later," he agreed.

"Shall we have another beer?" she asked, yet her arms remained fastened about his neck. Kissing her languid smile, he carried her to the refrigerator, which she like some unhinged robot opened with one drooping hand, reached in for beer. "For my strong man."

"Thanks," he said, carrying her and beer back to the chair, while she unscrewed the cap. She liked the stubby ones best, though her hand could not encompass them. That no doubt was why, he thought, and why while in the throes of her senior year at the student factory she took on part-time jobs to stretch her day, as much as her bank account. So once had he, of course, and Miriam. "My last check should be here soon," he said apologetically.

"Good, and I'm expecting one on Friday."

"Good." He reached across the table for a pencil, while she held her forehead with a hand too small to shield her morosely watching eyes. Now he tore a sheet of paper from a pad and placed it before him on the unimpressionable table top, copied addresses and phone numbers from the list he carried at all times in his wallet. He was leaving her his itinerary, not of places where he might be at certain times but where other people were already ensconced, the Seattle and Los Angeles offices of the driveaway, the Warman Bros. Studio, Brendon O'B, Miriam, his mother, his "publisher," etc. As a joke, he scratched out the F.B.I., the C.I.A., and the D.M.V. "Can you be at our phonebooth at eight o'clock on Thursday night?"

"Yes," she said.

"Now, is there anything else?"

"*Us.*"

"Forever," he said, kissing her crinkled lips. "Meanwhile anything more temporal?"

"Can we turn off the fucking radio?!"

"Quite." He leaned back so that she could reach the knob. "Bring the beer along," he said, pocketing his cigarettes. He carried her to the middle of the room and her free hand found the elusive lightstring somewhere behind his neck; they were halfway to the livingroom when the light went out by her remote control. In the livingroom he carried her to the front door so that she could snap the lock, then lowered her to the table lamp. Had he not pinched her rump the three-stage switch might have provided a five-act tragicomedy. Now they were in almost total dark, for that insomniac tug had aimlessly turned its back. In the narrow hallway, Irene rested her head against his chest while her feet and her lolling beer bottle thumped the walls. "I'll take that beer," he said before throwing her on the bed. This lamp he would handle by himself.

It took an embarrassing while, but Irene was not laughing when finally the light went out. "You're strong," she said.

"You're quite an armful," he did not deny.

"I'll get ready." She lay paralyzed.

"Ah, you want me to carry you in there?"

She shook her head. "I forgot to ask for a transfer when I got on."

"A kiss will do."

"Add that to your collection," she said, kissing him on her way by.

Things must not have gone altogether efficiently in there this time, for he was in bed drinking beer when she returned. This despite the fact that she had not so much to do, he knew.

"We're out of goop," she explained. "I had to use the foam."

Graciously overlooking her use of 'we,' he smiled and, "Ah. Old Slippery."

"Sorry," she said, climbing into bed on top of him.

He put down his beer and stroked her waist. They were going to do it this time speechlessly, the way she liked best. He only nibbled with his lips, leaving to her imagination what they said. Fingers, forearms, belly, thighs, in their own ways could talk, in languages she well understood and answered back. With her on top, it was like a luxurious swim before the dance. They could not sink, the gentlest motions held them up. Their bodies knew exactly when to roll, and when to beach, and as they did so he could feel a tapping upon his back. He paid no heed at first, but underneath him Irene grew tense. Someone was trying to cut in on them. "Ignore it," he whispered, redoubling his energy as he felt hers ebb.

She tried, bucked him almost fiercely once or twice,

but then collapsed. "Shouldn't we see who it is?"

"It's probably just a telegram," he hissed. The tapping became a pounding now, this intruder was a persistent one. "*Damn.*"

"You'd better see."

"I guess." Heaving off of her and out of bed, he found his pants and shirt. Tucking himself in as best he could, he leaned over to pull her covers up. "Stay warm," he said.

"Hurry back."

To begin with he hurried off. Ardor ran stiff interference for him in the half-lit hall, but that was flagging by the time he snapped on the outside light, unsnapped the frontdoor lock. This nervous man was new to him, though he wore the familiar cap. Behind him stood his faithful cab, its highbeam lights glaring warningly at George: My driver is a good, an honest man—be kind to him. In the brightness the driver's good and worried face sought to remind George of fond wife and kids back home. George smiled reassuringly, and the heartened man waved his yellow flag of truce. His breath was stronger than his voice. "Telegram for Irene Patterson."

"Ah, thanks very much."

Her messenger beamed relief.

"Do you want me to sign for it?"

"Oh yes!" The messenger fumbled in his coat. "Sign right here!"

Nodding, George obliged. He handed a quarter to the messenger along with the receipt and "Thanks!"

"Thank you, sir!"

"Goodnight!"

"Goodnight!"

When the messenger was lumbering well on his way to his steadfast steed, George turned off his own pale light, and closed and locked. He was shivering a little as he relayed the message down the hall to snug Irene.

"What now?"

"Telegram for Irene Patterson."

Wide-eyed, up straight, uncovered, Irene shivered too. "Me?"

He watched her tear open the envelope, unfurl the yellow sheet inside, grimace. He watched her face for further news;

57

finding none that could be readily translated, he glanced at what she handed him. "That's convenient," he said, returning it.

Irene threw the telegram on the floor. "You knew he was coming back for his things. I've told you that."

"I know."

"He still is my husband, after all. This used to be our house."

"I know."

She drew him down to her and kissed his head, on the bare top of course. "Do you mind very much?"

He shrugged.

"I could wire him not to come."

"Oh sure."

"No I couldn't—I don't know his address now. I could be gone when he comes."

"Gone where?"

"The movies, the library . . ."

"You mean the all-night branch?"

They let it go at that. Cuddled beneath the blankets, they fondled one another rather absently for awhile. He found her breasts warm to the hands, but slack. He was slack himself. "How are you feeling now?" she asked at last.

"A little tired."

"Me too," she said. "Do you want to sleep?"

"We could try."

They kissed. "I love you, George."

"I love you." He turned off the light.

"Maybe we'll wake up during the night," she said, patting his thigh.

He patted hers. "Maybe we will," he said.

THREE

They had not, he discovered at almost eight o'clock. In fact they had spent a profound night apart. Right on, old stud, *bien fait*. And now? His intent was to leave her filled with love, yet he found himself fondling her only tentatively. The truth was that he was already on his way. Before him the clock hummed on with ceaseless energy; beside him Irene awoke to catch him looking at her with something near impatience. She frowned, then arched her eyebrows questioningly. Remorsefully, he shook no. A smile flowed over her face, gently pinking it. "Then I dreamed we did."

"Oh, how did we do?"

Now her smile seemed to flow into her smiling eyes, sending little shivers through her body. "Mmmmm."

"Phew," he said, smiling too.

She kissed him softly on the lips. "See, we always manage to compromise," she said, jumping out of bed.

He laughed, and in the bathroom some minutes later he found himself shaving a still smiling face. But he ceased to smile when he started to put the razor back; he would be needing it. Without the razor there, Right Guard stood ensconced alone on their topmost shelf. He did not use the stuff, neither did Irene. Nor did they use most of the bottles on the next shelf below. Brushing his teeth, he searched the medicine chest for some token of himself. There was something very neutral about Vaseline; in any case, driving he would find use for that. Seeing nothing else of his, he returned his toothbrush to the rack. It was time he bought a new one anyway.

The bedroom cheered him up a bit. Even after filling his bag with spare shirt, shoes and socks, there remained ample evidence of him. Besides his tobacco, papers, cigarettes, etc., there were his odds and ends of clothes, his last year's mail, his books. The mail he put in his big blue Woolworth shopping bag, in a corner of the closet out of sight, then looked around once more. All things considered, not so bad. He shared this room beyond a doubt. It struck him that he had not owned pajamas of any kind for many years.

In the livingroom he swelled his bag with maps, paper and envelopes, pencils, pen. In the kitchen, Irene had filled a smaller bag with hard-boiled eggs, candy, and oatmeal cookies. "Ah, many thanks."

"Breakfast is almost ready," she said.

"Please, not much for me."

"You've *got* to eat."

He poured himself a cup of coffee, had lit up a cigarette when she placed a Three-Egg Cheese and Olive Omelet in front of him. At least, since she served it on one large plate for the two of them, he could take sly advantage of her good appetite. He took a big bite, to palliate. Watching her dig in, he remarked, "Well, give my regards to Pete."

She did not say, but asked, "Will you be seeing Miriam?"

"Probably."

"Will you make love?" She had stopped eating, but now she dug in again almost voraciously.

Would he? He did not know. On past visits he had, not so much out of passion as out of habit, quite naturally. This time, he could not foretell. Thus he did not ask, Will you? He toyed with their omelet instead, and then they put down their forks simultaneously.

He did not really want to go. He never did, he knew, of course, feeling his heart making an omelet out of his guts. Parting was always like this for him, had been ever since a broken family first played egg-toss with him at a fragile age; but now something further seemed to be happening. In the past he had simply accommodated his errant heart, accepting its gift of adrenalin as fair exchange, knowing he would want to spend that along the way. Today another possibility occurred to him: Stay. But looking down at Irene's little hand on his, he shook his head. "One more time!" he said, and wryly smiled, for he had heard his heart applaud those words before.

"You haven't *eaten* anything, George!"

"Oh yes, just right," he said, kissing her outraged mouth.

"Will you stop somewhere for lunch?"

"Oh sure."

"You haven't really got enough money, have you, George?"

"Don't worry about *that*," he said, leading the way into the livingroom. "Hallucinations of the future again," he diagnosed.

"Will you promise to stop soon and eat an egg, at least?"

"I promise, yes." He stood stiffly behind her with his bags, watching her unlock the front door and open it. Only then did he put down the bags with foolish care, straighten up to take her in his arms, feel their hearts applaud in unison.

"*Us*," she said.

"*Us*." Scooping up his bags, he hustled them out of there. He carried them half a block away before he turned to wave to her underhand, then hurried on again. Her little answering wave would finally have broken his heart, but for the gift of adrenalin.

He did not take the bus, but traveled free with the dogs and cats. He was not only saving thirty cents, he was storing up exercise. His driver might have been one of the friendly ones, besides, the kind who wanted to tell him what a nice day it was. The sky was blue, the sun was bright, a fresh breeze teased the fluffy clouds, etc. He knew. And besides again, the dog-watchers were not walking their routes today. This was payday for them no doubt, they were down at City Hall picking up their bi-weekly checks. While they were in town, they might as well drop in at Woolworth's, check out those new red caps.

Actually things were not so bad in town, even for a free-lance traveling man. There were two or three real faces in the bank, toward the back. George's teller let him have his cash, after consulting with the President. There was a fly on the candid camera lense. Ah, there went an armed guard to take care of that. Even so, another fly wanted in; George held the door for him. He himself was glad to regain the street. He blended in quite well out here, with his bags. People seemed almost to know what to make of him. A few girls did single him out, and he smiled appreciatively back at them. As a tactful gesture toward ladies and gentlemen, he did not stop to crack his egg just yet, though he was beginning to develop an appetite. He only bought a green toothbrush at Walgreen Drugs, by way of precaution and compromise. If things got really bad, he could suck on that.

Not in the Turner Towers elevator, he could not, for they had posted regulations governing such. For good measure they had a tall young executive who noted George carried nothing very current in his larger bag, excluding maps. The slender nostrils of such a man dilate, twitch; meanwhile he is pretending to hitch his hornrimmed glasses up. The little lady next-by notices the executive's nose, and sniffs. Lucky the traveler who has had a bath this week. If he did not belong to the Right Guard set, they could in good conscience object. In any case, he could only travel four floors with them, for he was in a hurry to take his next bath in Los Angeles.

The Quadruple-A OK Driveaway was located at the end of the hall, behind frosted glass that said INSURED WALK IN. In reality one squeezed, between the door and the scarred settee, which faced the gasping red-faced man hard at work behind the oldest desk in the West. Bill Bartko worked with sleeves rolled up and loosened tie, forefingers banging the tricky keys of a strange machine that miraculously punched small dents and holes into four sheets of paper all at once. Its shredded ribbon had probably come with the machine when he bought it new some thirty years ago; he had no real need of it anymore, having learned to type in Braille after a year or two. He had never bothered to learn to read it though, for he had an excellent memory. "Well there! George Alberts!"

"Bill Bartko!"

"Put down your bags!"

George did, and they shook well-remembered hands.

"Sit down, sit down! You're the writer. You're taking the little '66 Valva to L.A., for a Mrs. Gloria M. Stottlemeyer. I won't bother you with the address now, I've got it written here. She's in the phonebook anyway. She'll be there anytime after three tomorrow afternoon. You can use regular gasoline. Use 99 when you hit California. There's a forty dollar deposit, I believe I told you that," Bill Bartko said, and George spread four bills upon his desk. "I gave you a full tank. Save your receipts, she'll pay tolls and repairs. Is that all your luggage there? Good, she's got her trunk full of Presto Logs. Watch out for the cop in Cottonmouth. Try not to look Mrs. Stottlemeyer in the eyes—they cross. Her left rear tire is bald, the others fair. She's got pitmarks in her hood, I've marked them here. I'll be sending her a copy of this by air, in case there's any argument. She seems o.k. She's a nurse with the D.V.E., whatever the fuck that is. Death Valley Emigrants? You'll be traveling alone? Don't pick up any strays. How's your family?"

"All fine," George said.

"I'll have these forms made out in a jiffy," Bill Bartko said, punching full-speed ahead. "You may want to take a look at the map before you go. You've traveled the route many times, but there may have been some changes made."

There had indeed, and Bill Bartko had worked hard keeping up with them on his 1940's map on the wall behind George's back. Broad red crayon lines, ruler-straight, covered all but a few of the delicate, meandering tracks of yesteryear, marking the progress of the highwaymen. Blue lines cut wide swathes through what had been green and yellow countryside, blotting out whatever little lakes and towns had been in the way. White dots stood for the newer towns, the bridges, dams, and cloverleafs. The most recent additions were a tri-color splash where lately had stood some of the last of the redwood trees, and further south, a blotch of black and blue in the vicinity of Los Angeles. In total effect, it was the map of an army of caterpillars (*Laucania unipuncto*) on an acid trip. After a brief study of it, George felt real need of a cigarette. In deference to the wheezing breath behind the desk, he forebore. Bill Bartko would not have objected, he was sure, and that helped a lot. One can almost take pleasure in a nervous fit when not coerced. "How is the driveaway business these days, Bill?"

"It's a bummer, George. The insurance is smothering me. I lost another one this week, just two days ago. She sideswiped a semi on Snoqualmie Pass. Mrs. Brown of Browns Point, you may have read about that. Three children, luckily they were all at school. A nice husband—Mike—I met him once. Alice was one of my regular drivers, too, no drinking or pills or anything. Christ, it makes you think." Bill Bartko, wheezing, paused and thought. "It makes you wonder why you stay in this business, George. Then there's the State—they're trying to pin a carrier

63

license on me. I'm no carrier, George, you know that. They know damn well we don't employ our drivers, we let them drive our cars as a convenience to them, and to our customers. They know we can prove it to them by our books. Now they say they're going to put a new bill up before the House. The truth is they're trying to wipe us out." The telephone rang, and Bill leaned wheezing and listening into it. When he spoke, his voice shot out in impatient barks: "Where you going? . . . When? . . . What's your name? . . . How old are you? . . . Sorry, I don't have a thing going that way . . . No . . . How can I tell, maybe a week, maybe a month . . . No . . . No . . . *No* . . . Try some of the other driveaways . . . Yeah, thank you too." He hung up hard, sat for a moment glaring in front of him, at his map. "Christ, it gets so you don't want to send out anyone under twenty-five—or anyone over either. You don't want to send out anyone unless you know him well—and you hate to send out those you do." The big man turned bloodshot eyes on George, spoke with a wheezy wistfulness to him. "It's time I got out, George, don't you think?"

When George did not answer right away, Bill asked himself. "But what am I going to do? I've got five kids to support. My youngest wants an airplane!"

"Ah."

"It's a tough race, George."

"Yes, it is," he agreed. Wheelspun America, loathe to give way to the flyaways.

Bill ripped the forms out of his typewriter, spread them on his desk. "Sign here and here and here and here," he said, roughly jabbing each. Gathering the $40 in his big hands, he heaved to his feet and stood looking out the window while George signed, then waved George to his side. "She's the little black one," he pointing said. "Here, the white copy's yours," he said, carefully folding it. "Don't forget to have it signed, send it back in the stamped envelope. You're due in L.A. by Friday noon. You should hit Oregon by nightfall if you leave fairly soon."

"I'll be taking right off."

Bill Bartko handed him the keys. "Have a good trip."

"Thanks, I will."

They shook hands firmly, and George got his bags from the settee.

"I'll get the door," Bill Bartko said.

"Thanks." In the hall, he heard it wheeze closed behind him quietly. He took the stairs this time, preferring not to worry the executives, on so short a voyage. There were no regulations posted here, other than WATCH YOUR STEP—USE HANDRAIL. With a bag in each arm, George could not comply. Perhaps they did not have this well surveilled, except of course for fire and smoke. Stepping carefully, George did not light up, soon hit the fireproof door to the parking lot. KEEP DOOR CLOSED. It slammed itself behind him wickedly. Out up here were only a few high school boys, together with junior executives on morning break, surveilling their world from the pop machine.

"Hey, Dad."

Having nothing to buy or sell he waved to them underhand, headed for his blind date. She looked fit enough. He only glanced at her pitted face, but did check out her lamps: one of her highbeams was gone, but she could see well enough with her lowbeams and parking lights. Her left rear tire still wore a little stubble on it. Her doors unlocked, and after some coyness her ignition too. He strapped her buzzing belt behind his back. Now she was ready for anything. Waving to their matchmaker and to the boys, who lounged with congealed envy around their cool machine, he guided her down the ramp.

She must have been up all night; the man at the door asked for a three-dollar cover charge. She was starting out an expensive one, but he had ways of curbing that. One way or another, she would help pay her share. He already had in mind to camp somewhere along the road tonight, spend a few hours on her leather lap. He had to smile, for at just that moment the little Valva coughed. Had someone been adding ESP to her tank? He tapped her accelerator experimentally, giving her a couple of quick shots, and she purred Yes. She was a city girl, her license plates told that. Entering the freeway she balked a bit, but soon pulled out of her funk—anything to get back to Los Angeles. Now they had a pact: he would escort her safely to town in exchange for certain favors en route.

They took the first leg at conservative speed, fiftyfive, while he gauged her thirst. The freeway was posted so, for cars and trucks. It looked to be a real drag for cops, who streaked

65

by in search of fun. There was simply no sitting around waiting for trouble anymore, they had to go out and hunt it up. How they must be missing the good old billboard days, you couldn't even hide a bike behind these shrubs. No wonder their fleeting profiles looked so glum, Phase Three was making them obsolete. Soon they would go the way of the coniferous trees, recalled to mind now by their rotting stumps. Did they too peer nostalgically up at Mt. Veneer National Park, where the exterior decorators were hard at work?

George pulled over for a last long look at the breath-taking mountain top, still fringed by green below the sparkling white. I'll remember you well, he vowed, while the little Valva fumed. She was proving to be not a very thirsty one, but it was time he cracked himself an egg on her steering wheel. Ah, Irene had thought to include a little present of salt in his picnic bag, all wrapped up in wax paper and rubber band. Hm, didn't Miriam used to add black pepper in hers? That's all right, darling, I love you nonetheless well. Yet it did make things harder for a traveling man, remembering two wives at home, one left behind and one ahead. He did not dawdle over his picnic long.

For one thing he was anxious to investigate an oblong object up ahead. What looked strangely like a billboard to him. Yes it was indeed, right beside the road, as big as afterlife. WELCOME TO FORT LEWI, it plainly read in black and grey. He slowed down to savor it, and just in time. Even as he glided by, the sign keeled over quietly and disappeared. In his rearview mirror he glimpsed the chagrined face of a highway-man, his caterpillar ensnared in a guywire net. Creeping toward him through the brush was a patrol car bestrewn with broken boards.

A mile or two on waited a pretty girl, seemingly adept at evading traps. Seated comfortably upon her sleeping bag, she smiled and waved, but George and Miss V passed her up. They were bound on a different trip. Abreast they saw her soft face crimp twice, though in the mirror her shoulders shrugged. She knew there were miles behind and cars ahead; meanwhile she and The Mountain would meditate. Ascending the next grade George slowed down, and Miss V coughed. They were feeling belated pangs, for the pretty girl was out of sight.

66

They hit Oregon intact and with time to spare, Bill Bartko would have been pleased to know. A silver-haired toll-taker met them at the bridge, and though he did not smile he did say thanks. His manner suggested that they treat his roads with care; though they had not been invited, well-behaved strangers he could tolerate. Marked as a Californian, poor little Miss V seemed almost to slink. Of course, the glum streets of Portland encouraged that; she relaxed a little in the hills south of town. Now they could almost imagine they were back in Washington, but for that river running north. The Willamette was turned on for them tonight, rushing good tidings from the mountain tops. What, was there a party somewhere, did the hydraulic engineers have something to celebrate? Ah, there they were now in their big hip boots, reeling in.

The highway pioneers, in deference to their colleagues, soon left the river to them entirely. They had chosen a more challenging route, straight, wide, up. They had laid a four-lane path through these blasted hills, and they were most intent on using it. Miss V found herself encircled by a herd of orange brutes, each one signalling messages of emergency to itself; Caution Men at Work Watch Out. They were adhering strictly to their throughway code: the harder we chew on this concrete, the more time we can expend on its maintenance. The way was all theirs, for they had said their limited access prayers. Aha, what was that up ahead, a blasphemous rock? Caution! Caution! We'll take care of that! No no, rocks don't have feathers, they at the last minute guessed. Tread you, little bird! Now there went a deer across their black-topped park and crapped on it. Two eight-ton sweepers broke rank and charged.

George and Miss V escaped onto a limited egress path, for they had received a message from ahigh, in flashing red. EAT. They had stumbled upon The Highwaymen's Hideaway. Double rows of brutes guarded the place, front and back. A few had not turned off their blinks. Not himself one to be easily dispirited, George turned Miss V so that she did not have to look at the gaping, prognathous jaws. She could take comfort in all those as yet unconquered trees—there was a story to take back to Los Angeles. Patting her rear end on his way by, he headed resolutely for the enclave. Two bearded sentinels stood before the door, but they stepped apart at his salute. He smiled

67

inside, for their leader had saved a place for him. The slender girl behind the counter looked up in real surprise, at sight of a fellow-pagan and human being. Actually these knights-errant didn't look so bad with their visors up; a few had even taken their plastic helmets off. The ones on either side of him withdrew their elbows an inch or two, allowing George to almost fit in.

The worried girl still seemed unsure. "Coffee?"

Smiling, he nodded please, and thanks.

"Menu?"

"Thanks," he smiling said, but on opening it he became less sure himself. Giant Hamburger 100% Pure Beef did not look quite good to him, after some months without, nor Hot Chili Con Carnivorous. He settled finally on Bacon, Lettuce and Tomato with Pickle and Potato Chips, by way of compromise, and almost of appetite. Pardon me, please, Irene. He stepped to the men's room while his bacon cooked, for it was time he set his morning coffee free.

The gallants had spent plenty of the taxpayers' time in here. The floor was clean, but the walls were littered with signs of them. Meat me at 9:00 p.m., stall 2, George faced—6 or more inches only. Checking his mental clock, he hurried his coffee along, and quickly flushed. Washing his hands, he eyed the Eau de Cologne machine, between the Nylon Comb, the Sanitary White Handkerchief. The one heroic symbol in this place was the fourth machine, and he dropped a quarter in that. It worked! A gift for Irene in case she was still out of goop —if not first for Miriam.

It was 8:47 when he came out; some of the boys had left. Two were outside jacking up in the parking lot. George sat down with the remaining malingerers, who eyed him askance. They must have heard the clink of coin, heard the Trojan drop. Certainly the girl behind the counter had. Her pale face was now alight. She handed St. George his sandwich with something like reverence, and with his pickles crossed, and sat on the hot chocolate machine to watch him eat. From a kitchen hole a wrinkled, weathered face peered out with the mistrustful eyes of a husbandman. Farther back and to the right, George could see wrinkled, weathered elbows working methodically at the sink. Nearer by, he could almost see the farmer's daughter's cunt.

"Can I warm your coffee up?"

"Thanks!"

Blushing, she gave him another pickle too, a larger one. Reseated on the hot chocolate machine, she stared at him even more openly. He was getting more than his quarter's worth. He chewed his Bacon with Remorse, for how was she to know that in his thoughts that rubber already was stretched for two? Under other circumstances he would have been delightd to take her outside awhile, introduce her to Miss V. Certainly those lovely cheeks were softer, warmer, more penetrable than leatherette. Finishing the last of his Pickles and Potato Chips, he left thirty cents by his plate and smiled a well-earned apologia.

Little Miss V coolly awaited him. In her rear view mirror she had noted his faithfulness, but also his appetite. She was feeling a little empty herself, if the truth be known. Her quivering needle attested that, and her cough. It should come as no surprise—how many others had he known with a range of almost four hundred miles? She had carried him almost a third of the way to Los Angeles; meanwhile he had eaten twice.

> He happened to have
> a mathematical mind
> One doesn't know why

Stroking her soothingly with his toe, he wheeled her into a Pay-and-Go, where the tourists lined up impatiently waiting to be uncapped. Spotting California tags, the chief himself approached. He would need to see cash or credit cards. George flashed his roll, with smile. His SSN? George flashed his smile again. References? Well, he had a book "published" by Happers, and the chief did not read quotation marks. He did take the precaution to examine the serial numbers on George's roll before turning to an aide-de-camp: "Give him ten!"

Gallons or dollars was that? This youth didn't look like a likely one; George held his peace while Miss V lapped up regular, continued to hold it after the youth put his nozzle back. "Ah," said the youth, and ran off to fetch his change from a plastic garbage pail. Out on the highway again, Miss V was half-full at least, and George had a Handy Three-way Opener for his eggs. Now too, they had Oregon more to themselves, most of the highwaymen having decided to call it a night. Their abandoned brutes crouched cold and wary beside the road.

69

The deer and the rabbits frolicked around them now, and no doubt the mice. Whenever Miss V interrupted them in their play, they paused to stare back at her reflectively: they wanted to know if she was one of the orange ones. George waved to them reassuringly, and Miss V hummed. Thus they bid farewell to Oregon, for the chief had given them enough gas to get out of state.

At the border the California trooper stuck his big round hat in George's window, looking for vegetables. Hm, did they count Presto Logs? The trooper went around back with George to have a look, probe among them with his torch. What was George trying to do, remove Birnam Wood to Los Angeles? But yawning he soon waved him on: Phase Four would take care of that.

George waved hello to 99 for Bill, and turned on the radio in quest of Jay. Musak seeped. He spun awhile—not a word of news. Finding music now, he left it on, for company, to keep Miss V and him awake. The rousing chords of *Finlandia* seemed to roll off Miss Shasta looming ahead. Over her white-clad western shoulder the moon peered almost full-faced, but the President wasn't coming through too well tonight. The refulgent peak was straightening out his refractive light. George saluted her. He knew her environs quite intimately, having observed them one summer from a fire tower in New Mexico. That year the forest service radio had picked up the Shasta signal more often than the Cibola, a refraction as fascinating as it was frustrating, for Calfornians are more garrulous than New Mexicans and Navajos, have more fires and rattlesnakes. More lady lookouts too, who finally became superfluous to a New Mexican shacked high up with Miriam.

"Let it rain, let it pour, we don't like it anymore." It left some wondrous memories though, of virgin trees and stars, in translucent air, which allowed one a lucid view of the hypocritic days below. He and Miriam had quite consciously savoured it; it had left an indelible love stamped on the heart, before a vaccine was discovered to counteract that. For Janet it had been almost the first taste of life, three pure summers' worth, many moons. She had been born under a more nearly substantial President, whose Western Farm House was in Show Me Land, and who had no ambition to be the Laugh in the Moon.

70

Tonight, here on Earth, boys and girls ranged the road. Some were plodding south, but the majority reclined on their packs with a thumb or big toe in the air. They were bound for Los Angeles or Marinland, young migrant worriers trooping away from home in search of a Family, or People across the sea. Never before had he seen the like, at night, excepting one evening on the road to Cantabrigia. Perhaps only because of the narrowness of the right-of-way, those hikers had stayed on their toes. They had been mere mass and silhouette dimly picked out by the little Anglia's candle power, until, around a bend, appeared a heavenly vision, her absolute blondeness illuminated by a halo all her own. Kids going home from university for the weekend, the driving professor had explained, passing the angel by. Soon later he had led George into a roadside inn, which they had all to themselves while drinking twelve percent stout before a five-hundred-years-old fire. Thus had they broken their journey through the midlandian freshets to the delta of despond. Tonight he passed up the inns, looking for the angel to reappear. Meanwhile he was in no mood to abet little girls; he would have been more likely to help them north toward Canada, where hikers still left the road to camp at night. They would do well to turn around at once, from the looks of things on 99. The few coming from farther south ran in what looked dangerous packs, their faces distorted by the hint of fangs about the mouth.

Perhaps he had been spooked by the music on the radio, a love song from Hollywood's latest Children Only chiller. With a flick of the wrist he exorcised Miss V, turned on her heater with another. Ah, old Bill had been right about the cop in Cottonmouth—there he went now, mooning by. His roadside audience cheered him on. Gliding away from the city limits, George put two more towns behind him before pulling off to give Miss V refreshment in Red Bluff. The youth was alone this time, and shaking: clearly he had not volunteered for night patrol. George came out smiling, to ease anxiety. Now it was his turn to be shaken, at sight of the posted price per gallon; he ordered half a dozen. "Yes, *sir!*" The relaxed boy became loquacious, and relaxed all over Miss V's windshield until it glistened, so pleased was he to have civil company. He was a real rambler, this one, soon became right boastful. His station had been held up more times than any other north of

Sacramento, twice last night, etc., etc. . . By the time he finally waved George on his way, George had to take care to drive around him. But on the road again he really missed him, enough to turn on the hellish radio.

". . . your late late happening, Jay Gardner, folks, on KOO, member of the NAB courtesy of the FCC. Sponsored tonight by Sleepy, the little pill that wants to be your ever-lovin bed companion. Take two or three at bedtime—take four or five, as directed. You'll love the little devils. But hold off a few minutes, folks, I've got a confession to make, I owe you folks an apology. (I tried, George.) I've been allowing too much time to the Bleeding Hearts and Pacific Doves, overlooking you Real Folks out there. I've been home the past couple of days listening, to the tapes, adding the hours up. It comes out something like three to one in favor of the Bloody Liberal Crackpots. Tonight we're going to give equal time to the Realfolk—no Innovators or Revisionists allowed tonight. I hadn't realized how many of them had infiltrated us—I'm sorry, Folks. They have a way of sneaking up on you in the night, catching you with your phones down, so to speak. Let's turn on the lights, pick up those phones and have a ball tonight. This is the first day of Pluviôse—let's celebrate! Call 415-330-2200 right now, Folks. Let us hear your intrafamily problems. Are you getting enough help from the Government? Satisfied with the way old HEW's handling your compensation and relocation? Getting any runoff from your Congressman? Call now, Folks . . ."

Spotting an abandoned sentry box, George derouted to seize and occupy. Miss V remained behind to observe the troops and monitor the Folks. This was a lucky night: he found an open line and had ready change enough. The phone rang but twice.

"KOO. Yeah?" The Switchboard operator had a switch-blade voice.

"May I speak to Jay Gardner, please."

"What's with this 'please'? You drunk?"

"Not at all. Tell him George Alberts is calling long distance, man."

"He knows you?"

"Ya, through the mails."

72

"What do you want to talk about?"

"Life."

"That ain't enough."

"O.K., I want to wish him Happy Pluviôse 1st."

"Where'd you say you were calling from?"

"Somewhere outside Red Bluff."

"Hold the line a minute, man. What's your name again?"

George Alberts still. He added up at least a minute's worth of creak, grunt, and beep. Then, "Never heard of him!" Jay Gardner called into the telephone.

Hanging slowly up, George saw Miss V eyeing him solicitously, and she opened a sighing door to him. She had heard. In fact her quiet manner suggested she had heard more than he. She seemed to be offering him her lap, but he put a few miles between them and the sentry box before taking her up on that. He chose a well-lighted parking lot, drew her up beside a handsome laundry truck. She was a steadfast one, albeit cool at first. Some might call her a Revisionist.

FOUR

A tapping at the window came, through a thin layer of plastic sleep. Things had happened overnight. Hands had shriveled into claws, wrists had shrunk to skin on knobby bone. If those were living knuckles, they had lost all sense of pain. In fact this girl looked to be a drop out from a post-graduate funeral school. Dolled up in her wedding gown, or the finest from her bottom drawer, she had clearly been waiting a long time for morn. From beneath her kerchief a few dry wisps of hair escaped, trailing her liver spots. Farther down, in front, a scattering of lesser hairs had sprouted long ago, perhaps to replace the missing fangs. Her *neck* . . . And yet, her old eyes had a glint in them, her smile a surprising gap-toothed winsomeness. Her voice had zest: "Heading *South?*"

"Not right now!" he called, closing out the sight of her.

"That's all right, young man, you get your sleep. I'll park over by the barber shop."

Up on a sleep-numbed arm, he watched her saunter gimpily to the shop, park herself against the pole like some ancient candy striper waiting for them to open The Tonsorial Surgeons' School. One shied from imagining what distractions she carried in her big cowhide kit, what her deep red shawl was for. He gave her a few minutes to go away or decompose, then sat sighing up to awake Miss V, smoke a cigarette while she warmed. Still there, the apparition waved to him pluckily from her pole. Resignedly he waved back, rolled his window down. "How far you going?"

"Mexico!"

"I'm not going that far."

"I'm taking it in little hops," she said, hustling gamely over. "I'll be stopping at Berkeley first, then Hollywood."

"Aha." He hoped Bill Bartko would forgive him this one,

in memory of the trotaway. "Hop in then," he said, opening the door for her. "I can take you as far as Sacramento. I have to stay on 99."

"That's all right, dearie," she said, stashing her kit and shawl between them on the seat, smoothing the laps of her traveling gown. "I've got time. I'd be in Berkeley now if my car hadn't broken down in Lewiston, but that's all right. Those are bad hills they have there, you know. There's no way out of town but up, unless you want to go northwest and all around."

"That's Lewiston, Idaho?"

"Yes, she refused. I can't say that I blame her much. She was due a rest. She's a 1925, and the roads were softer then. The young man who towed us back up the Snake gave me a handsome price for her, I thought. Said he collects antiques. That's encouraging, isn't it? A nice young lad, he was, with easy ways, his hair not too long in back. About here, it was." About kerchief length, or Washingtonian. "He gave me sixty dollars for her, and refused to let me pay the towing charge. Can you calculate a young man like that, in this day and age?"

"Well . . ."

"Well, it will pay for my bus ticket in Mexico. I won't trust myself for hiking there. I hear there are bandits down there, and I don't know the lingo well. They say the busses have air conditioning. My lands, will you look at all the boys and girls. I had no idea. I couldn't believe my own eyes last night. I haven't been so crowded since the Fourth of July parades back before the war, back in Juliaetta. Oh, my sakes," she cried, pointing at the bald head of a girl going north. "I suppose that young girl had to sell her hair? She did have a little baby on her back, it looked like a cute little tyke, I think. Did you see its face?"

"Not clearly," he said.

The old girl turned forward again, patted her kerchief straight. "I believe I'll like Mexico," she said. "I have nothing against foreigners, you understand. Once I get the lingo straight, I expect I'll feel right at home down there. In the meanwhile I'll just feel my way. You can tell a lot from a person's face." She gazed out Miss V's window rather glassily. "It's just when there are so many of them you get confused." Now her eyes turned to him, and he took a quick look as they

75

began to turn warm and wet. "I used to know everyone," she said.

"In Juliaetta?"

She nodded yes.

He nodded too. "It's a pretty town," he said.

"Yes, now it's time I traveled a little bit, now the girls have all left home. I've always had a notion to see the sights someday. Oh, I've been to Spokane and all around, but never anyplace you could rightly call real far. Spokane is big, but it isn't real foreign-like, not after you've been there twice. I read a lot. I love to read the travel books. That's not quite like seeing for yourself, of course. Oh, I've always had a notion to see the sights." She was getting a good opportunity right now, for they had been slowed down by a little town at the edge of a shopping center. "Maybe I'd have enjoyed them more a few years ago?"

"Yes," he said, but after a glimpse of her face he quickly added, "There are still some lovely places."

"Mt. Shasta was a marvel last night, wasn't she!"

"Yes, she was!"

"I can't wait to see those mountains in Mexico. You know, the ones with all the p's and t's? Yes, I expect I'll be seeing my granddaughter down there."

"Ah, your granddaughter lives in Mexico?"

"Oh yes, she's a regular traveler, that one is. Canada, New York, Grand Rapids, New Mexico. Ha ha, in my last letter I called her my little Mexican jumping bean. You know how they are."

"Yes, I have a daughter in Canada."

"My Belle visited there. Oh, she's a lively one, that one is, and a beauty too. I've been just a little worried about her lately though, to tell the truth. Her letters have been seeming a little strange to me. A little mixed, I mean. She used to have a lovely hand, like me. Oh, it's probably just an old lady's fancy though. Belle's probably as fit as she can be, just feeling her way. 'And youth, of course, must have its fling, tra la la la la . . .'" Her la's trailed into a coughing fit, which she softened with an embroidered handkerchief, then dabbed her streaming eyes. "A touch of pleurisy," she diagnosed. "When we grow older, our lungs congest. When we don't have full use of our

76

lungs, we use our stomach in place. Remember that, young man."

"I will. Thanks."

"As I was about to say, tra la, Belle's all right. She's got a head on her. She was right at the top of her high school class before she left. She's always been a brainy one. Athletic too. She could have been a champion tennis player—she was second seed in the Northwest Tournament, in Yakima, at the time she left. I'd like to have seen her finish her schooling, myself. Sixteen is too young to know what you want. I blame it mainly on her young man. He's a Scientrologist, you've heard of them."

"Ah, I believe I have."

"Oh, she'll be all right, she's good at heart. Her mother didn't have a lot of time to spend with her, of course. She's been so busy with her work. My Helen has always been like that—a forward one. She has the biggest chain of beauty parlors in Alhambra now, and owns her own apartment in Hollywood. Doesn't she know the famous ones, the stars and all! You'd never guess!" With a little smile and shaking head she paused long enough for George to guess, or for her to recall their names herself, or to study their sons and daughters slouching north. "Doesn't it look warm out there!" she said, tucking her handkerchief into her cuff. "That next town ahead is where you said you'd drop me off?"

"Sacramento, yes."

"You know, if you was to drop me off somewhere in town I think I just might take the bus. I think I might like to feel my way down here a little bit, and save my gown. I suppose there would be a bus to Berkeley everyday."

"Oh yes, more regularly than that. I'll show you where the Greyhound station is."

"Good, I'll just take the bus. When I get there I'll give Grace a ring, maybe she'll come pick me up, if she isn't busy with an office call. If she's busy, maybe one of the children will come after me. Ah no, they're all away from home just now. Mary is a singer (she's seventeen now) and Linda is in Chicago doing social counseling. Linda's two years older, nineteen now. Maybe little Danny's back. I hope he is. He won't be able to drive, of course. He broke his two legs in a motor cycle race out

77

East last week. He always was a high-spirited one. He'll be twenty-four now. We used to have great times, him and I, when they lived up north. They used to come visit me from Spokane right often in the summertime. That was before Grace divorced, before my Harold died. We still had the variety store. The children used to love to help Harold stock the shelves and wait on customers, even little Mary did." Coughing lightly, she dabbed her lips and eyes with a corner of her handkerchief this time. "Well, if Grace is busy she'll probably be able to tell me how to find her place. She's a psychiatrist, you know."

"Ah." He hoped he looked duly impressed, for her eyes shown with pride plus something less positive. But sight of the Greyhound station brought them alert; she leaned forward to peer at it. "Here we are so soon, and we've scarcely had a chance to chat." She turned to him. "What line of work did you say you're in, young man?"

"I write."

"I could have said! For the magazines?"

"Mainly novels nowadays."

"Novels! What's your name?"

"George Alberts."

"George Alberts . . . Haven't I heard of you?"

"Probably not."'

"Have you had a book printed yet?"

"Oh yes, but none of them have sold very well."

"Well, I know you write lovely ones. I'll have my eye out, be sure of that."

"Thanks very much."

She put her hand on his. "Excuse an old lady for going on so much."

"I've enjoyed it a lot."

"No, don't get out. I'm used to doing for myself," she said, adjusting her shawl and hopping nimbly out. "Thanks for the lift!"

"I hope you find Belle all right."

"Yes, and I hope you write a best-seller book."

He laughed, she laughed, and their laughing eyes kissed in space. He watched her limp briskly off, turn to smile and wave at him. When a busy man let the door fly closed in front of her, she turned to smile and wave once more before shouldering it. She was a swinging one.

78

Miss V herself was far from pleased. Now that she had him alone again, she pinged with pique. She had heard. She had seen them holding hands, on her own lap. Sakes, yourself, that's no way to keep a pact. She'd been around. That's not the way a fellow treated a lady in L.A. Shamed, contrite, George checked her dials: it was time he took her out to lunch. First he had one other stop to make, at a curbside bank. That had looked much like U.S. currency floating across the street, on an inshore breeze. Now in the mirror he could see it fluttering along a granite wall, in search of a deposit slot. An unusual town. Munificent, free. Scrambling he acquired the bill gratefully, though it turned out to be a lowly one. That was quite all right, quite just: new in town, he did not wish to overdraw his account.

To tell the truth, he was impressed. Generally shy of banks, he had to admit this restructured Bank of America did have merit. It seemed only right that he invest his money locally, encourage the economy. He stopped at a handily located Piggily Wiggily branch, purchased a quart of chocolate milk on which to float an egg. Now he felt himself a viable part of the community, but poor Miss V was suffering. They had already passed several three-star lunchstops up. He was looking for something less glamorous, more befitting the modest investor that, after all, he was. Thus he pulled in at Serve-U-Self and filled her up at marginal cost. A well-balanced package, particularly for the longer term: she seemed satisfied, and he had become part of the labor force. Time enough later to compound their capital gains.

The prospects looked less favorable out of town, leukemia was spreading fast through the countryside. Bill Bartko had plenty of updating to do on his chart. They were laying an eight-track trail alongside the little four-laner he had known, blooming superstructures thrived in his American River bed. Far to the east, on one of his green patches, loomed a mighty, lonely bridge waiting for a highway to climb over it. Patience! Patience! Your time will come! Meanwhile George decided to make good use of his, passed a smug, high-walled viewpoint up. He could have his brunch on the run, drink his chocolate milk before it warmed, crack and eat his egg, with salt, Irene. In this way he might be able to wrap things up in time to take Miss V out on the town tonight, before getting her home by

Friday noon; first he would ask some help of her, for this was a business as well as a pleasure trip. She seemed agreeable. Passing rather slowly through Modesto, she sailed past Merced Madera Fresno Tulare and Delano, stopped for a quick drink in Oildale. Then it was up past the Tehachapis, down past the Topatopas, into the Valley of San Fernando and Hell's Angels.

They took cover in a classic motel still called auto court, with a fine old lean-to for Miss V. The proprietor had built all this himself, when he was younger. He didn't work that hard these days, but he tried to keep things tidy. There was enough to keep a man amoving, without the missus. Over the years he had collected quite a bunch of big old door keys, which confused him sometimes. They all looked the same—exactly. Well, No. 3 wasn't really locked that much—with his *passepartout* boot he kicked it open. He handed a key to George. Inside was cozy. Partially modernized though not remodelled, the room had new draperies. Besides the big bed and chair and dresser, there were a little stove and ice box. A big glass ashtray from Las Vegas graced the radio. There was running water, hot and cold, and in the shower stall a fancy paper bathmat from Hawaii. The phonebooth wasn't half a block away, the proprietor boasted. All in all, though perhaps not the one Billy Wilkinson would have chosen for him, this place was quite a find, well worth $4.50. The proprietor earned that much finding and filling out his receipt and guest books: the missus used to do that.

George and Miss V paused to rest a moment before getting down to business. She seemed to like her little lean-to, and behind George's draperies it was cool and quiet. They had the place almost to themselves, they had noted: no other autos, but in front of No. 5 two motorcycles, small ones, probably non-belligerent. Without too much worry, George left Miss V to rest a little longer, while he took advantage of the 24-hour telephone facilities.

These worked, and Miss Warman Bros. Goodafternoon had heard of Billy Wilkinson. That it took her ten minutes to locate him was probably not significant. He *sounded* enthusiastic.

"Hi! Sorry! George Alberts?"

"Hi! Yes."

"Billy Wilkinson! Are you calling from Washington?"

"No, from outside Los Angeles."

"Terrific! Can we send a car for you? Are you at the airport?"

"No, out in the Valley."

"Have you a place to stay? How long will you be here?"

"Yes, but not very long. Until sometime tomorrow probably."

"Oh! Well, let me see! Are you free this afternoon?"

"Yes."

"Terrific! Hold on a minute!" He was gone scarcely longer. "How about four o'clock?"

"Fine!"

"You're driving?"

"Yes."

"Terrific! Go to the main gate and ask for me—I'll phone down that you're coming!"

"Great! I'll see you at four!"

"Yes! At four!"

With things working out so well, George paused to light a cigarette before calling Brendon O'Brien. Brendon O'Brien was not at home just now, but he had left a recorded message.

"Hello, this is Brendon O'Brien. I'll be working on location today until about five-thirty. Please leave your name and message, and a phone number at which I can reach you. Thank you for calling. Brendon O'Brien."

The phone fell silent, then beeped encouragement, or impatience.

"Hi, this is George Alberts. I'm in Los Angeles for a day or so and hope we can get together. I'll be busy this afternoon, but I'll call you as near six o'clock as possible. Goodbye until then." The phone beeped thanks, or re-encouragement. George hung it gently.

By no means discouraged, he hurried back to wake Miss V. First he had a bit of cleaning up to tend to, some small unpacking. No. 3 was quick to look quite homey. His bag looked well upon the dresser, his eggs fitted in the ice box snugly. He placed his salt above the stove, for dryness, his cookies and candy inside the cupboard, should it be mouse-proof. He approached the greyheaded toilet apologetically, for it had seen many years of unrequited duty. Understandably, it sighed a lot, but flushed one more time, coughing rather dryly. As for the basin, water trickled from both faucets with about equal warmness, a study in compromise and fairness. With help like that it did not take him long to wash the soap and shave his face. In the livingroom he thought to congratulate the ceiling light, which smiled back at him quite spunkily. The broken-hearted radio had died with Caruso. It seemed to rest a little easier when George moved the Las Vegas ashtray to the dresser. Now he could in all good conscience go to Hollywood.

Miss V was ready, leapt from out the lean-to smartly backwards. Was she trying to taunt those cycles? No question but what she knew her roads and freeways, seemed to follow them by sense of smell alone, snuffing blood and oil and gasoline with rapture. Perhaps sight of all those locals also fired her, if indeed she could see them, so densely were they farting. Close above their heads hung the fart of yesterday, stirred gently by the aerials. Yet she swayed gracefully among them, unfazed, light-hearted. Slowed briefly by the backwash of a five-way no-fault fender-denting, she nonetheless got him into town ten minutes early. Time for a cigarette, tinged very lightly with nostalgia. Those hours spent tramping up and down outside this fortress had been in a fresher air, with one or two true companions among the troops, but in the long run no more productive than all those hours spent within it.

The main gate had been refurbished, a catatonic sentinel stood newly planted where had been the bougainvilaea. It asked and answered simple questions, then excused itself while its programmer searched its brains for Billy Whatsisname. Oh, there had been changes, but few improvements, a returnee noted. The door burped twice before it opened, then clicked its teeth behind him. An armed man led him up carpeted stairs, down a carpeted hall, to a harried girl, who rose from her dictaphone to offer tea. Mr. Wilkinson would be right down, she apologized, and excused herself, no doubt to type a note of that.

"I believe I'm a little early." The teacup, a fragile one, did not quite fit its saucer, more fragile yet. The result was chatter on the verge of clatter. Ah well, George felt himself steady enough by comparison, and the noise helped a visitor to appear impressed. "There've been a few changes made," he said.

"There certainly have," she agreed. "Have you worked with Mr. Wilkinson before?"

"No, I'm not in the business. I happen to know Warman Bros. from having been a reader here, years ago. I doubt that he was around here then."

"He's in his early twenties," she said, suddenly looking several years older than that herself.

"Not likely then."

"They bought the studio a month ago, and they've been firing the old staff all over the place. The girl I've been working with for two years got her notice this morning and went home early. I've got a bad cold, I should be home myself. There's almost no one left."

Here came one now, armed with a grin, uniformed, in tight striped pants, tight but flopsy-collared blouse, sandals meshed, amen. "George Alberts?"

"Billy Wilkinson?"

"Yes! You're just in time to meet Roland Rollins! He's upstairs! Bring your tea!"

George followed Billy Wilkinson up another flight of stairs, followed rattling down a grander corridor or hall. This was territory never explored by Screen Story Analyst, and Billy Wilkinson stopped at the grandest door. After a moment of beaming silence, he swung it wide. If they had hoped to surprise someone inside, George for one was disappointed. Where had all the Producers gone? Had no one thought to buy them along with the studio? Was no one to inherit all this elegance, no one to command the massive desk, no one to fill the mahogany chairs, no one even to pretend to wield the gold pen and pencil set?

Perhaps they had thought this room was a movie set. They had paved the deep-napped carpeting with plastic. The draperies, older than George's and heavier, were drawn. All of the lamps were lit. The life-size portraits looked at one another with heavy, old-fashioned pride, but into the gold-framed mirrors with embarrassment. They knew that this room was theirs alone, but even if someone were to prop them in their chairs they could not talk, for they had gone back to the silent film, and were its stills.

But now someone did appear behind the desk, taking up the entire width of it with a kind of airy massiveness. He wasn't so much propped or sitting in the chair as balanced on the arms of it. This claimant had golden curls and flowered, flopsy-collared shirt. His grin was boyish crocodilian. His bulging eyes were bright with business schemes and movie plots. He did not use the gold pen and pencil set but waved his own, red ballpoint. In his other hand he held George's book, in Penguin reprint, here blown up to quarto size. "Hi there!"

"Hi there!" Billy Wilkinson said.

"Hi!" George said.

"I'm Roland Rollins! Glad to meet you, George!"

"Glad to meet you too!"

"Sit down!"

Billy Wilkinson plumped onto nearby mahogany, and George eased rattling next to him.

"Sorry I can't be there in person, but cable's the next best scene. I'm winding up some dealies in London, won't be in L.A. until Saturday night. I hear you probably won't be in town very long this trip."

"No, probably not."

"Well, let's get right down to cases then, see if we can wind this up. We like your book. *I* like your book. I've only read this far"—two thirds, he showed George where his foot-long forefinger divided it—"but I'm convinced it could be made into a terrific film. Those two old gents are marvelous—I have in mind Wayne Hudson and Newton Rock. I'd like to see Joe Lemon or Nichols Nichols direct. For little Mary I think of Diana Black or Leslie White. We'll find a top cameraman. I'd like to get Billy's brother, but let's not bother with all the details at the moment. We'll be working with a budget of two million dollars, to begin with. Any questions?"

Roland Rollins sat back and Billy Wilkinson turned to George with eyebrows raised enquiringly, no longer grinning.

"Well," George said, "mainly I'd like to know how much of my book you'd use, how faithfully you want to translate it."

"Oh, faithfully, faithfully! For openers we'll want to shoot the New York skyline on location. Then we'll zoom into the turtle bowl. We'll be cutting in and out a lot. I'll be honest with you, George, we won't be able to use every word of your

84

novel, every scene. It would make too long a film, for one thing. We'll have to zip it up a little. Kids just won't watch anything that moves at a slow or lifelike pace anymore. For my own part, I wish it was different, but it isn't. We've got to think of the audience. I think we can make a film the kids will really go for—so many of the old gents' problems are exactly like their own. Exactly like the blacks' problems too—we'll want to bring all that in too. We'll bring in the women's libbers, the gays, and so on. Let me jot that down. But we can go into the details when we get the gang together. If you've seen *Swing High Sweet Harriet* you have some idea what we've been up to lately. I'd like you to meet with the producers and director soon, so you can get a picture of the people who will be working on your book, catch their angles. I know I wouldn't want to put a book of mine into the hands of just anybody. Does all this sound reasonable for starters, George?"

Roland sat back again, and Billy's brows arched higher. George quieted his cup and saucer. "Yes, I'd like to meet them. You can understand my concern for the well-being of my novel. I like it very much as it is, that's why I wrote it that way. I think it could be made into a lovely film without too many changes. I used to be a story reader here, so I have some sense of these things. There's a film script right in the book—it wouldn't be necessary to wring one out of it. Most of the dialogue, for example, could be used verbatim. Perhaps the pace could be speeded up just a little bit at the beginning, but not too much—I think almost anyone will watch a naturally paced story if it's truly funny, human. In this book the pace grows gradually faster, until the scenes are literally flashing by, in the last third of the book especially."

Roland was jotting with his ballpoint, but quickly looked up to see George and Billy waiting. "Terrific! I was sure we could get together! We'll want to have all your thoughts, George. Let me just run over a few ideas I've jotted here. If you want to sell the book outright, I picture a twenty thousand dollar package, ten on signing, ten on completion. Now, if you'd be interested in working with us, I picture that same twenty thou for the book, another twenty thou for a preliminary script you'd write, forty thou more if you're in on the final script, and another forty thou if the film is actually

85

completed and released. That adds up to a one hundred twenty thousand dollar package, doesn't it?" Roland leaned forward now, and Billy looked to George.

"Yes, I believe it does," George said.

"That covers all the usual rights, of course: serial rights, TV, reprint, etc. We'll want to put the book out in inexpensive paperback, under our own imprint. I picture an edition of one hundred thousand to begin with." Roland leaned back, tapping his ballpoint thoughtfully against his lower lip. "Any other questions, George?"

"Are TV serial rights included in that package?"

"Naturally! Why do you ask that, George?"

"Well, I sort of shy away from a TV serial, of this book especially. The book has a pretty strong anti-television bias, you know—I'd hate to see it used to make nonsense of itself."

"Oh, I see," Roland Rollins said. "Well, I think we could exclude those rights in this case, don't you, Billy? Don't worry, we'll get around it somehow, George. Billy will get our lawyers working on it right away, have them work up a couple of contracts for you to look at. That will give you a few days to decide which way you'd like to go. We have your address, we'll have it off to you early next week. You don't have an agent, do you, George?"

"No, I handle everything myself. By the way, I think in my last letter I mentioned the possibility of a smaller outright payment, in exchange for a small percentage of the profits. How does that look?"

"I talked it over with our lawyers. They say such clauses are as good as meaningless—no one ever gets any take on the profits, unless he's a Hemingway or Brown, someone who can hold producers up for an iron-clad contract. You understand that?"

"Yes, I guess I do."

"Terrific! Well then, shall we call this a tentative agreement, George?"

"Yes, tentative," George said. "I have one other person to see while I'm here. I wouldn't want to promise anything until I've had a chance to talk to him."

"What company is that, George, may I ask?"

"As a matter of fact I'm not sure what company it is—I

believe it's a small independent. The man I've been corresponding with is Brendon O'Brien."

"Brendon O'Brien," Roland Rollins repeated, with a fuzzy smile. "That's the actor—he played in that last dolphin film, *Chicken of the Sea*. It flopped. I worked on a film he had a bit part in a few years ago. The other night I was at a party he came to. I recognized him and was going to say hello, but he didn't even look at me. I don't trust actors, George." Roland grinned, and George smiled, and Billy grinned. "Before I forget to mention it, I've been trying to get your new book from Happers. I wasn't able to get it through the bookstores, so I ordered it from Happers direct. I've written them three or four times, without success."

"You trust publishers?" George grinned; Roland and Billy too.

"Will you send me a copy? Terrific! O.K., I think you'll do better to go with an established company, George. These independents have more brash than cash, mostly. We'll get a contract off to you that should satisfy anyone, unless one of those hard-ass purists like William Faulkner. If you have any questions about it, just give me a call. If it looks right to you, zip it on back and we'll get going. Fair enough?"

"Fine," George said.

"Terrific! Very good to meet you, George! Take care of it, Billy! See you, everybody!"

"Right on, Rol. See you!"

"See you!" George called.

They remained seated while grinning Roland Rollins faded, tapping George's book with his ballpoint. Billy Wilkinson turned to George. "Terrific, isn't he?"

"Isn't he?"

"It's a little late—I'll catch the lawyers in the morning. We'll get things zipping! Done with your tea?"

"Yes!"

George followed Billy Wilkinson downstairs, returned his cup and saucer with thanks to the red-eyed lady, who mumbled something. She almost stuffed the saucer in her purse, and had her coat on. In the corridor Billy grinned. "We're just getting settled here!"

"I see!"

87

"It'll be terrific working with you!"

"Yes!"

"If you have any other questions give me a call!"

"I will!"

They shook hands at the foot of the stairs, while the guard looked on. "See you, George!"

"See you, Billy!"

Returning George's nod and some part of his smile, the guard triggered the door for him. It clicked more quietly this time. The uptight sentinel hummed "Take Me Out to the Parking Lot," a Warman Bros. tune. It was too early to catch Brendon O'Brien, so George took Miss V out for a quart of oil. For himself, after waiting for some big fumbling boys to count their food stamps out, he bought a Big Time candy bar, sat munching on that in a Piggily Wiggily parking lot. After all those calories, he bought a package of cheese crackers for protein, Irene (Hi, Pete!), washed that down with a pint of half-and-half—for vitamins, Miriam. Then he leaned back to enjoy an after-dinner cigarette, catch the five-thirty news in the parking lot, which seemed to be on long cable tonight, or telestar, so dim was the image on the fuzzy screen that he could scarcely discern the events, let alone the personages—something about a hunger march, it seemed. At six o'clock he found himself a quiet phone in front of a wax museum.

"Brendon O'Brien speaking."

It seemed to be a live voice this time, but George hesitated a moment before responding. Then, "Hello. This is George Alberts again. How have you been?"

"Good to hear your voice, George. I received your message. I was working on location until about five-thirty. How long do you expect to be in town?"

"Until sometime tomorrow probably."

"Until sometime tomorrow."

"Yes."

"Can you be more specific?"

"Probably I'll be here until mid-afternoon."

"You definitely won't be here tomorrow evening, is that correct?"

"Probably not, yes."

"You aren't sure?"

88

"I'm quite sure, yes."

"Good. Then what are you doing this evening?"

"I have no plans."

"Can you come over to my house?"

"Sure, I'd like to."

"Very good. When can I expect you?"

"Well, would around seven be convenient?"

"Around seven this evening will be quite convenient. We'll have a bite to eat and some talk. I look forward to seeing you then."

"Can you tell me the best way to get there?"

"You have my address?"

"Yes."

"Where are you now?"

"Near Alameda Avenue and Olive Boulevard."

"Good. You'll be heading west. First go east on Alameda Avenue 1.8 miles to Golden State Freeway. Turn south on Golden State 1.11 miles to State 134. Go west on 134 5.0 miles to US 101. Go north on 101 1.4 miles to Laurel Canyon Boulevard. Turn south on Laurel Canyon 3.2 miles to Mulholland Drive. Go west on Mulholland 2.9 miles to Coldwater Canyon Drive. Go south on Coldwater Canyon 1.7 miles to Preview Drive. Turn left on Preview 1.6 miles to destination, on the right. It's blue brick. Shall I repeat that?"

"No, that should do it!"

"Have you got a pencil?"

"Yes!"

"You'll be heading west—"

"Fine, fine! I think I have it!"

"Do you think you have it?"

"Yes!"

"Better check again to be sure."

"Yes, I have it!"

"Have you got paper too?"

"Yes! Yes!"

"Very good. You'll be heading—"

"Yes, fine! Yes! I'll be on my way now! See you soon!"

"Ho, very good. I'll see you soon. Thank you for calling."

"Thank you!"

"You're very welcome. Call again."

Hanging up quickly, George broke out of the booth, not so much for air as sanity. Miss V looked rather sympathetic. After a calming cigarette, he perused his paper and chewed his pencil. He was tempted to visit that wax museum instead, but sighing deeply he turned on Miss V and headed east on Alameda.

To conserve adrenalin as well as sanity, he might not soon remember the way over there, which included quick stops at the Skeleton Shack and Engine House No. 202 for new misdirections. Preview, man? I really dig that—come in a minute while I get my pants on. . . . No thanks very much, I'm a little late already! I'll try that firehouse on Mulholland! Preview Drive? *Preview?* Hey, Charlie, isn't that in Pasadena? . . . Naw, not *Pasadena*—try Santa *Monica* . . . Thanks! Thanks! Yet he finally made it there in spite of almost everything. The brick box was blue indeed, with white scalloped roof in half relief. Stuck halfway up a wooded hillside, it was surrounded by a large cement yard, or fire lane. A cement drive, straight and almost perpendicular, climbed to a ten-foot notch marked PRIVATE PARKING. Gritting her teeth, Miss V clung on. Those scallops looked almost real from here, or were they abalones? A ramp, much like a children's playground slide, led from the parking notch to a doorway. It was steep and slippery, but had a railing. Luckily George was wearing rubber soles; no cowboy could have made it. Up on the landing he glanced down at Miss V for admiration, but she was too busy clinging.

"Come in, George," a voice called. "The door is open."

Smooth and knobless, the door swung inward before he could push it, and snapped its teeth behind him. He found himself in a shiny corridor, also slippery.

"In here, George, I'm in the swimming pool."

George made his way cautiously down the corridor toward a distant sound of splashing. Doors along the way were clearly marked in stenciled letters: KITCHEN, PANTRY, PUMP ROOM. The door marked POOL swung outward toward him. When it swung closed behind, he found himself on a narrow catwalk in semi-darkness, and grabbed a railing. What light there was in here was under water. At first he could make out little but the shadow of a swimmer flitting here and there in graceful figure eights and circles; gradually the shadow gathered substance as George's eyes adjusted. Sleek and solid, it seemed to have no trunks on. Now with a wriggle of hips it leapt entirely out of water, hung glistening in the air quite shamelessly for a moment, by way of confirmation. Arching backward, it cut the surface of the water cleanly. The splashing was itself applauding, and George was sure that it was not he himself who chuckled. With a careless swish the swimmer glided over to the catwalk, lulled in the shadows at George's feet, treading water. "George, it's good to meet you."

"Brendon O'Brien?"

"In person. Did you expect me to be taller?"

Dimly George could see the face now, a narrow glint of smile or snappishness about the mouth. If that was a recorded voice, the dolphin was a clever actor. "Did I hear you speak, George?"

"No! I'm glad to meet you!"

The dolphin flipped a flipper coolly. "Same. Did you have trouble finding me?"

"No no, very little!"

"Very good. Shall we have a bite to eat before we get down to business?"

"Well, I—"

"Good. You'll find some mackerels in that basket. Toss me one, will you?"

"These?" The bucket writhed with gasping bodies, twenty-five or thirty of them, in murky, sloshing water. After some tentative groping, George grabbed one by the tail and tossed it.

The dolphin leapt high, caught the squirming mackerel neatly with his pointed teeth, and swallowed. "Very good," he said, applauding. "Toss a little further this time."

These mackerel were packed in mackerel oil, not water. George grabbed another tail and flung it. The dolphin shot across the pool, made a flashy catch just before the mackerel hit the surface. Gulping, he applauded. "This time higher." George flung one at the ceiling. He watched the flipping, flopping arc of it high across the pool where the patient dolphin waited arching backwards, almost in the bleachers. Sliding gracefully into the water with his catch, the dolphin applauded loudly. Those bleachers were built to hold a crowd of several hundred. "Not quite so far," the dolphin called, and George dropped one from the railing. The dolphin really had to race to get it. "Have a bite yourself, George," he said, applauding.

"Thanks!"

"They're imported from Prince Edward Island."

"Thanks, I've eaten!" Maybe if there had been a little soysauce . . . George flung a big one at him. The dolphin caught it in the face this time, had to juggle a bit before he swallowed. "Nice shot. There are vitamins in the KITCHEN."

"Thanks, I had a Big Time bar and crackers."

"There's cod liver oil in the PANTRY, if you're thirsty."

"No, I had a pint of half-and-half!"

"O.K., then let's get down to business," the dolphin said, relaxing on his back. "George, I think your book is beautiful."

"Thank you."

"Call me Brendon," he said with a little shiver, almost a wriggle.

"Thanks, Brendon."

"I think your book is beautiful. I like its human qualities," Brendon said softly. "Do you know what else I find in your book, George?"

"Humor?"

"Pathos, George. And do you know what else?"

"Irony?"

"Cross-impact. I don't think I've read another like it. It will make a beautiful script, George."

"Ah."

"Any feedback?"

"Not just now."

"George, it's Brendon."

"Not just now, Brendon!"

"Then let's get down to business, George," Brendon said. "I have in mind a middle-range budget, in the order of seven hundred and fifty thousand dollars. We'll work outside the unions—I'm damned tired of hiring fifty extra hands every time we move our tanks and cameras. I want to see this beautiful story presented simply. No big stars or anything. For the old gentlemen I'd like to get some unknown actors. There are plenty of fine actors no one has ever heard of—Los Angeles is full of them. Of course, we'll get a top-notch director. I have one or two in mind. George, any feedback?"

"Well, Brendon," George said, "I agree this book would be best be presented simply. I like that approach very much. I wonder how much of my book you would want to use, how faithfully you would translate it into film."

"Faithfully, George, very faithfully. I think your book is beautiful. Naturally, no film can ever follow a book exactly, to the letter. It simply isn't possible. Certain changes simply have to be made, you understand that. For example, we'll want to change that turtle to a mackerel. But essentially the film will follow your beautiful book, in spirit. Any feedback?"

"Not at the moment . . ."

"Then let's get down to business." Brendon rolled over on his stomach. "I have in mind a purchase price in the order of ten thousand dollars. That includes all rights except TV serial, which you mentioned in your letter you did not wish to grant us. I've talked to my lawyer and he says we can handle that. He's writing up a contract. You also mentioned that you would like a clause granting you a small percentage of the profits. I've talked to my lawyer—we can put that in. I think you mentioned five percent. We'll make it ten. Any feedback?"

"I wonder if you would want some help in the writing. I've given it some thought lately, and I think I could turn the book into a good and faithful filmscript without much trouble."

"George, you're a very good writer. I mean that, George. I happen to have a writer of my own—we've been working together for years now. He's put together some excellent scripts for me. I know you'll like his work as much as I do. I also have my own cameraman—you'll like him too . . . Any feedback?"

"Well, speaking of cameramen, I've wondered if this book might not best be filmed in black and white. It would seem appropriate for a story about two old men—"

"It wouldn't be possible, George. No one would buy it in this day and age, not any more. Besides, we'll want the mackerel to show up well, the greens and blues. Speaking of the little devils, will you toss me one?"

George tossed one hard and high. "I've got to be going," he called as Brendon snapped it up.

"It's an agreement then?" Brendon asked amid applause.

"You mean tentative?"

"Can you be more specific, George?"

"Let's say we have a tentative agreement, Brendon."

"Beautiful. I'll get that contract right off to you," Brendon called, flashing through the brine. "George, one more before you go?"

George threw two. "Catch you later, Brendon!"

"Beautifwullll," and bubbleful.

The POOL door flashed open in front of him. He hurried incautiously along the oily hall, almost slammed into the outer door. Swish, snap, he was out of there, inhaling the smoke-choked air. Beneath, Miss V crouched low in her PRIVATE PARKING notch, with clinging tires and pained grimace. She was not amused when he slid down to her on his rear end, and she squealed with fright as he backed her slowly to the street. On level ground at last, she sighed, and they headed east on Preview Drive. They headed north 2.0 miles or more to Ventura Boulevard, where a phonebooth awaited them at 20:00 sharp. Providently, he had three-minutes' worth of Piggily Wiggily change.

Irene was at her station, her voice sounding far away and very young. "Hello," she said. "I love you."

"I love you too. How have you been?"

"All right. And you?"

"All right. But you don't sound too sure of it yourself."

"Oh no, everything is fine. Patter and I have been leading a quiet and uneventful life. Where are you calling from?"

"L.A."

"How was your trip?"

"An easy one. Has there been anything new up there?"

"Not a thing. No mail at all—not even any telegrams."

"How is Pete?"

"No different. He didn't stay long—we had a fight."

"Congratulations, ma'am."

"I thought you'd appreciate that. Have you a place to stay tonight?"

"Yes, an old motel, a cozy one. I think you'd like the looks of it."

"How is your money holding out?"

"Very well. In that way it's been a lucky trip."

94

"But not in other ways?"

"I'll tell you all about it when I get home. At least I've seen everybody I planned to here."

"Were any of them interesting?"

"Oh yes!"

"Have you made any decisions yet?"

"Nothing definite. You should be getting some contracts soon."

"Do you want me to open them?"

"Yes, why don't you see if you can make anything out of them. Meanwhile, you could send a copy of the Happer book to Roland Rollins c/o Warman Bros. Shall we make a date to talk again at the same time on Saturday night, 8 p.m. your time? That way I'll be able to call at night rate no matter where I am in the U.S."

"Yes. George . . ."

"Yes?"

"Have you heard any *other* news?"

"Not a bit. Jay Gardner is lost."

"I heard. There's been nothing else on the radio. I'll buy a paper tonight."

"Good luck with that—"

"Your three minutes is up!" broke in a peevish voice.

"*Us.*"

"*Us.*"

Together they gently cradled their phones, and left their booths. They both headed west, but George stopped off at a 7-11 store, for beer and newsprint. Irene would have wine with hers. At Sepulveda Boulevard he turned north. Darkness had settled in, compressing the smog a bit. He turned Miss V's wipers on, as though removing the scum might help. In any case, there was little to be seen at night, though those did look like blinking red lights ahead. Yes. He guided Miss V carefully around a bevy of cops—gathered together for a flashlight test? No, in their midst a commuter lay on his back, bleeding his life onto Sepulveda. His shoes were off, his knees were up. Blood gushed from his heaving chest, only his face was white. Once past, George turned Miss V's applauding wipers off. She seemed to take all this in stride, and hummed. Hm, she *was* a cool one, wasn't she.

He was glad to be home again. Leaving Miss V in her

95

shed, he gave his front door a kick, carried his cold beer to the icebox top. After taking off his shoes, he lit a cigarette and inhaled a beer, standing up. Then he carried another to the bed, beneath the plucky light. The Las Vegas ashtray was within easy reach. Cozy, almost relaxed, he went in quest of news, three cans' worth. Irene would find whatever he had missed. He threw the paper across the room, good company for the radio. From the kitchen, a pretty little mouse waved her tail goodnight. Waving back, George dropped to bed, and slept almost as profoundly as Enrico.

FIVE

He awoke in borrowed light, his shrouds were not quite opaque. Leaning out of bed, he parted them. The sun was in deep funk. Difficult to say what time it was, somewhere between six and noon or noon and six. He thought to shave and shower, in either case, for the sake of Mrs. Stottlemeyer: better to be late than rank. Naturally he wanted to try out his Hawaii mat. Beautifwull, the way it worked. The greyheaded toilet too. Nor did it take a man long to eat an egg, two mornings out; packing got a little easier in every way, day by day. One sad note: his ceiling light, for all its pluck, had given up. He blamed himself for having asked too much of it last night. Well, at least the ashtray looked satisfied; it had had a blast it would not soon forget. No sir, they weren't making many live ones like George these days . . . With a fond Aloha he departed Lucky Three, leaving the key in the door for the proprietor.

Ms. V was sharp. She revved all the way to the wax museum (what had been blood on Sepulveda now looked like chalk) and churned on a while after he turned her off. Ow, she slapped his wrist when he felt in her cubbyhole for Bill Bartko's braille. It was all on the paper, as Bill had said; George went over it quickly while he smoked a cigarette. Mrs. Stottlemeyer, nurse to the Death Valley Emigrants, was expecting him by noon, sure enough. Ms. V was crowding her 1400 allotted miles, what with that detour to the PRIVATE notch—every extra mile would cost him twenty cents. It was going to be close, with luck. Hell, he'd back her into Los Angeles if it came to that. Parting he slapped her rump. His booth had been fumigated overnight, it was littered with quiescent bugs. The telephone company charged him twenty cents for that.

"DeeVeeEee Hello."

97

"Hello, is Mrs. Stottlemeyer there?"

"Thiz iz Miz Stottlemeyer speaking."

"Ah, I'm George Alberts. I've brought your car down from Seattle."

"How is my car?"

"Just fine—she behaved beautifully all the way."

"*She?*"

"Sorry! He or it!"

"Well, where are you now?"

"Near Alameda Avenue and Olive Boulevard."

"I'll be out in the field this morning, down in Downey. We're at Imperial Highway and Paramount Boulevard, fourth trailer on the left. Have you got a pencil?"

"That's all right!"

"When shall I expect you then?"

"What time is it?"

"Why, ten o'clock."

"Hm, it may be slow going. Does noon sound all right?"

"We close at noon. Don't be late."

"I won't! Goodbye!"

"Goodbye."

Back on Ms. V's lap, a glance at her map told him there would be about a five-mile overlap, a dollar's worth. Having picked up an extra one in Sacramento, he decided to play it straight ahead. They headed east on Alameda first, *then* south on 5, sometimes known as 101. Where it intersected 60-70-99 and sometimes 10, he took all four sides of a cloverleaf, for luck, and arriving Downey knocked on a wooden door to boot, forty-fourth trailer on the left. He knew where he was because someone had thought to stamp D.V.E. on it.

Inside, a young girl shrieked hysterically, as though he had raped her with his boot. There followed loud thumping on an interior wall, and guttural, unisexual grunts. The girl shrieked again in unfeigned agony. George rapped with his fist this time, and utter silence fell. The door swung open as though by its own choice; now someone took its place. "Who are you?"

"George Alberts. I—"

"Just a minute. Don't come in." She was neither young nor old, pretty but with the sharp, enclosed face of a parakeet. Her hair was straight and smooth as jet. She strode through another, interior door, which she slammed not so much behind her trim back as in George's face. Everything was fine, she just had to thump her head against the wall a few more times. She was, one might say, smiling when she reappeared. "Where is my car?"

"Out here."

It took her no time at all to recognize Ms. V, for all the dust, and now she set out on a sharp-nosed inspection tour. There were still the four tires, four doors; yes, there was the steering wheel. One lighter, one ashtray, one chubby cubby-hole, one kleenex rack. One crumby lap; she scarcely glanced at the cleaner one in back. "You brought my logs?"

"In the trunk," George said, handing the keys to her. "I suppose they're a little hard to find down here?"

"California has a high forest products tax," Ms. Stottle-meyer said, counting Presto Logs. "We need these for our family cook-outs on the beach."

A glint in her crossed eyes discouraged him from pursuing that just now. "What is the D.V.E., may I ask?" he asked instead.

"Department of Venereal Ecology," she pronounced, slamming the trunk lid, flashing her little flopping braless breasts.

"Oh! I've been wanting to ask someone about the pill."

"We don't deal in contraception," she spat out, "but in prevention only: group discussion and therapy, film persuasion, sex re-education, hypnosis and medicines." Her sharp glance asked if he would care to try some of that himself, match head-thumpings, parakeet beaks perhaps. "We've declared war on compulsory pregnancy."

"I suppose you work mainly with girls?" George asked.

She beaked yes. "Six to sixteen years of age. Lower to median economic and privilege range, lower capacity and achievement range. I guess you want your ongoing deposit back?"

"Thanks! Do you find you're getting good results?"

"Stunning. Last year sixty-five percent of our girls remained heterosexually chaste. Our projection shows that ninety-two percent of those will not revert." She was in a hurry now, for the girl inside of the trailer was shrieking for some help. "Just a minute, Noxzema, wait!" Ms. Stottlemeyer shoved George a wad of bills: "I took out the dollar for the gas, and the three-dollar cover charge. It's really a dollar twenty, but . . ." She shrugged her little breasts.

Very generous. "Thanks!"

"We all must learn to bend, now and then."

"Oh yes," but let's not double up. "Sign right here, please."

Ms. Stottlemeyer went over the paper, every hole and slash, while Noxzema shrieked. Satisfied at last, she stabbed it with her pen. "There you go."

"Thanks again!" Parting he slapped Ms. V's flank nostalgically. "She'll want some gas," he called, but Ms. Stottlemeyer was deep in shriek.

Alone again, he strolled the Downey boulevards. He did not fit in. Down here, the citizens did not look, they watched. Here were not even the saving girls. These maidens cased one another with dark and red-rimmed eyes: intra-sting. As though beguiled, he made for an asexual booth. Naturally, he did not fit in. He tried another, older one, and that did work. He called the nearest, the Downey branch.

"Hello? Hello?"

"Hello. Have you anything for New York?"

"I can get you to Miami or Winnipeg."

"No thanks!" He tried the Montebello next.

"Hi."

"Anything for New York?"

"Nothing going northeast. How about Las Cruces, New Mexico."

"No th—what kind of car is that?"

"A '68 Impala Stick."

"No thanks."

"O.K., I'll fill up her tanks."

"Well—what's the deposit like?"

"Can you have her there by tomorrow night?"

"I guess so, yes."

"Don't worry about the deposit—get over here!"

"All right."

Montebello was scarce a twenty-minute trot away. Moving so, he attracted attention less, the slouching citizens watched

100

too late. It was the shavetail police dogs that noticed best. They sniffed George's bag, savouring his remaining egg, which reminded him of Irene's candy gift. Slowing, he delved for it, a Pay Day bar; he savoured every crunch. Well-trained, the dogs stepped curbside to drool out their hearts.

"George Alberts?"

"Yes."

"I filled her tanks."

"Many thanks!"

A white-haired man with a neat red mustache, he refused to look distinguished in middle age. "You just delivered a car for AAAAOK?"

"Yes . . ."

"All we'll need is your thumbprints and photographs." He led George to a curbside booth, where three cameras flashed. "Thumb this."

"Anything else?"

"Take 99 to El Centro, then 80 and 8."

"You bet."

"Here are your keys and contract. Don't wait for those photographs."

"All right." Now if he could find a '68 Impala Stick . . . "What is that, a race car?"

"Yeah, someone goosed her up for drags. You'll want to lean hard on her clutch. Have a safe trip!"

"Thanks."

"She's got extra duty torsion bars, but she still doesn't always corner well."

"Is that right?" George was leaning on her clutch—let those corners wait!

"*Floorboard* her!"

Floorboard her yourself! George meanwhile leaned on her with both his feet, and off they leapt in roaring low. Letting her corners wait awhile, he held her straight, since she was heading east. Soon he leaned again; second gear was more amenable. Third was another stubborn one, but urged by a two-footed lean she shot off in hot pursuit of a cruising cop. Hey, officer! Leaning hard on both brake and clutch, one foot apiece, he eased her back down to second gear and cautiously cornered her. She took that pretty well, in fact she seemed

101

quite sharp. Sighing, leaning on everything in sight, he eased her curbside for a pit stop. When he turned her throbbing motor off, she belched. She? It, for Ms. Stottlemeyer. Lighting a shaky cigarette, he checked his map on a rigid lap. Highway 99 crossed somewhere east.

"Let's try again, old pal." Conserving energy, he started off in second gear, crept around the block, testing the corners out. On the main drag again, heading east, he settled in behind a smoke-screening bus. It was high noon, according to the radio, time perhaps for news. Not quite: See *High Casserole*, a Roland Rollins film, tonight on Channel 8; meanwhile a few highlights from the score. George tried another station low on the band. At times he tended toward the dolphin, those greens and blues. He estimated he would be paying Miriam a midnight call tonight, assuming he found 99. For once he wished she had a telephone; somehow he did not have the heart to send her a telegram. In lieu of that, he leaned into third. Suddenly the track was clear ahead; the startled Greyhound had suffered a heart attack. That would teach it not to smoke so much. For himself, George fired up a low-tar cigarette; what he craved was the nicotine.

He was twice fortunate: unlike Ms. V, the Impala was eager to get *away* from L.A. Nose down, tail up, it charged onto 99 in fourth. George leaned back for a change, but did not relax. Somehow he felt conspicuous. Maybe it was the Impala's rakish lines, maybe the heavy padlocked wires that kept its hood from flying off. Maybe it was the way it howled at cops. In fact the only inconspicuous thing about this beast was its coloring, brown and dirty white. In a trackless desert it might pass unnoticed; Highway 99 was still six-laned at Kilometer 80, and fenced, for this was a limited access desert. At another time, George would have loved this space. He almost loved it now—but suddenly they were passing through Siren City. George leaned hard forward, shifting down two gears, to growling second. If the bawling cops took notice, they were all too busy figuring the local traffic out.

But at the edge of town stood one on foot, propped up by a telephone pole. He signalled for George to stop, swung open the righthand door, stuck his head inside. "Thanks very much," he said, tossing his suitcase in back. He slid in next to George and slammed the door. "All set," he said, waiting for George to start up again. "Sharp little car you've got."

"I'm just delivering it."

"I don't usually travel this way," he said, taking his plastic helmet off. "I usually fly, but that's no way to see the countryside. I borrowed this getup from the prop room. So far it's been working very well. Are you heading for Mexico?"

"Old Mexico? No, I'm going to New."

"Good, you'll be passing through El Centro then. I can pick up another ride before I cross the border. I'll just stop all cars until I find the one I want—I'd rather not try my luck in Mexico. The propman couldn't find a good Mexican outfit, not a recent one." He dropped his gun. "They were all out being cleaned, and I'm rather in a hurry. I'm out scouting film locations, you understand."

"I guessed you were probably in that line."

"I'm a cameraman," he said, removing his polaroids, hanging them in his mouth while he looked for a handkerchief. "Our next project will be low budget, in the order of a half million dollars, but I'm terrifically excited about it. I think we have a real sleeper on our hands this time. Heaven knows we're due for one."

"Do you often film in Mexico?"

"When we can—the light is good, for the greens and blues. Steinbeck started it back in '39. It's a good way to beat the unions too. I happen to be union myself, but I don't mind free-lancing on the side. We've got the producers by the balls—we'll just squeeze twice as hard next time." Smiling grimly, he held his polished polaroids up to the light; he had a steady, bloodshot eye. "Nice light out there," he said, and whistled softly. "Beautiful. Get that shot there." A semi-trailer, on its back, spilling plastic garden hose upon the desert. "We could have used that for our credits, if only I had brought my camera."

"You'll be shooting the entire film in Mexico?"

"No, we'll probably shoot the first few feet in New York. I don't know where we'll zoom into the mackerel bowl, probably in Hollywood. Then we'll pan down to Mexico. I couldn't bring my camera along, you understand—you wouldn't have been able to see my gun. Shit, I could have strapped it on my back!"

103

He whacked the dashboard with his fist. "I knew this was going to be a bitched-up trip! Oh well, I'm getting paid per diem and ancillaries—I make them sweat. If I can just make that connection in Cuernavaca, won't I sing! Meanwhile I don't know whether my computerized passcard will fit down there—it will in Mexicali, I expect." He inspected the card, held up its holes to the light. "I'll remember to get my tequila there. The Torreon J.C.'s did send me one of their cards, but I don't know how far that will carry me." He studied a larger, roundish one: TORTILLAMATIC, S.A. *marca registrada.* "It *looks* all right. You can't ever be sure of these Mexes though. They'll charge you ten pesos to snap their grandmothers—that's one reason I didn't bring my camera. This way they'll think I'm just like any other gringo bum. If I get in a tight grip, I'll flash my union card. No spicka da spick! We've been a prenotification company, as far as that fits in. When I come back loaded next month, won't they open their mouths and eyes!"

"You expect to start shooting next month?"

"The sooner the better, on a budget like this. As soon as we get a director lined up, we're ready to go. We've already lined up the old gents. Both beautiful kids, right out of the pen. We'll shoot them in black and white, save our color film for the greens and blues. It's cheaper that way, and it helps the audience to distinguish the story lines. What is this, El Centro already?"

"Yes, it is." They had stopped, for it was time to assuage the Impala's thirsts.

"Time sure pans when you get talking, doesn't it. Hey you must run across a few stories yourself. You deliver cars as a full-time thing?"

"No, not quite." George was watching the pumps; a junior economist, the boy was using two nozzles at once.

Not one to be easily distracted, the camera was collecting his belongings. He put on his helmet, adjusted his polaroids. "The name's Zoomer White. If you ever run onto any good story lines, drop me a line at Rollins Dolphin, Hollywood, or c/o Manhattan Towers, New York." He adjusted his gun. "Take care!" he called, and waved as he zoomed in on a telephone pole.

At George's window the boy stood waiting with outstretched

104

hands. George eyed premium dials, counted out half of Ms. Stottlemeyer's ongoing roll. The boy returned a dime. "Have a nice day!" he called, trotting off.

George lowered all the windows, bathing in the warm air of Imperial Valley. What was the Impala howling? *Faster, faster!* A roadsign announced YOU ARE 100 FEET BELOW SEA LEVEL. What were those smaller letters—watch for dolphins? Keep on laughing! Don't worry, Irene. Don't worry, Miriam. Don't worry, people. It's bound to hurt a little at seventy miles an hour. He waved reassurance to a tractor driver. The man's answering wave struck his heart, for suddenly he wished he were traveling ten years slower, back in the clean air of the bean and berry fields with Miriam and Janet, trading good work for honest dollars. I could hop from here to Cape Horn on either foot, with whatever load, he had written to a friend, professor and poet. Where was he teaching this year, in Buffalo? Probably. Where was Mr. Manzanita, still growing sweet raisin grapes in Fresno? Was Frenchy still boss of the beans in Watsonville? And Antonio at the other park? Not very likely, any of those, with the *braceros* locked out by the unions. Probably the Mayor of Villasoledad still got through though. How else could a hombre maintain his office; every canasta of beans bought a bottle of mescal and another vote, with enough left over for the fiestas and gas for the mayoral limousine. Was it still the 1950 Cadillac which he rebuilt himself in wintertimes? Smiling, George turned the Impala's radio and lighter on. Keep looking forward!

They were out on the unreclaimed limited access desert once again, patrolling the border line. The Impala felt ready to jump the fence. George was a little itchy too, having written the best parts of two books down there. He had used the beans in much the manner of the Mayor himself; every canasta bought a paragraph, with enough left over for beer and tequila and gas to get home again. What held his attention now was the Hermosillo radio, on which an excited voice was sputtering news or the name of a song. Something something hay tomado la luna, it sounded; then the quivering air went still and the mariachis took over again. That was one reason he had liked writing down there, he never knew exactly what was going on in town, could concentrate on the future for a while. *La luna, hay tomado?*

105

Entering Arizona they lost an hour, were overtaken by darkness and the Yuma radio. George pulled off for a pit stop here, a tanker of gas and a visit to the machine shop. The menu tonight was baloney or rattlesnake on rye, washed down by Spurt or Gila venom. USDA Choice. The change machine took a ten cent tip for that, and George and the pumper split the ongoing roll. The Impala had a black stripe across its back, he had forgotten or failed to notice. Behind the wheel again, he rolled the window against the cooling air, just in time for the better business hour. Due to the rapidly changing business environment, these men were placing heavy emphasis on the emerging markets and the merging markets. The further purpose of the readjustment was to more effectively utilize the resources of the aftermarkets. Ongoingly, that's where the emphases were being placed . . .

A few miles from town the emphatic voices faded out, to be replaced by the soothing clatter of country musak. For the first time today, George relaxed. In the moonlight the quiet cacti breathed Good Evening. Here and there a bypassed town beseeched. GAS—GAS—FOOD—EAT. Muggins, Sentinel, Pedra, Snurr, on the divided road to Gila Bend. It was on the edge of town that he first picked up the big sedan, parked beside the road with four or five heads in it. He had noted it as a matter of course, but paid little heed until bright lights moved in on him. He slowed down, for the road detoured here onto one of the older ones, while the highwaymen built anew.

That car slowed too, so he moved out—gradually at first, not wishing to challenge anyone. The lights hung on. They lit George's head and shoulders up, and surely the Impala's stripe. It was a lonely feeling, which musak could not soothe. Leaning hard, George took off. As the lights receded, he took a big breath and locked his doors. Those lights zoomed in again. This was a thin two-lane road made for Model A's, made obsolescent by 1950's Thunderbirds. It had old-time bends, around old houses, mostly dark. George cornered carefully but without letting up, and for a moment he and the Impala were alone again. "Good job, old pal!"

They were too soon in light; George let it come. "Go ahead, pass me then!" They were in an open stretch. The big sedan pulled abreast, and they hung together inches apart. The cowboys hung on as they approached a bend; George hung too. Neither one backing off, they took it so. Where in hell was everyone! They roared together into another stretch. Now the sedan began crowding him toward the edge, a sandy strip between road and ditch. George fell back, and the crazed boys on his side leaned out their windows to wave frantically at him: Pull over! Pull over! Theirs was a race car too, and they wanted his. "No thanks!" he yelled, and cut quickly left. *Floorboard* her! He was past them before the driver could get his brain unlocked. Pulling away around the next bend, he saw car lights ahead and leaned on the gas pedal with all his weight. For the first time in his life he prayed for a cop. In vain . . . Whoever it was crept into his ditch. In the mirror George watched him creep by the sedan, whose lights were not receding as much as George had hoped. He was asking of the Impala all he could. The stupid panel light did not work, and George snapped on the overhead light: the needle quivered at 110. He turned off the light. The lights behind were hanging on, but now he saw a red tail light ahead. With a laugh and a sigh, he zoomed in on it.

This lonely driver was rolling home at about 35. George settled snugly in back of him, letting the stiff muscles of his legs relax. The lights behind zoomed in, spread wide as that demented driver sought to mount the Impala's back. "Come on, let's get out of here!" George yelled to the one ahead, but that old man was suffering from overcaution or a heart attack. He would not budge. Nor would George, for all the prodding in the back. "Go on and ram me, dopes!" They chose to pass instead. When they began to crowd him, George fell back fast. There waved the frantic arms again. "No thanks, you silly dopes!" Giving up on him, they swung in front of the other car and waved at it. "Keep going, old man, keep going!" George pled, and waved him on. The crazy ones in front pulled off the road, and the poor old fool drew up in back of them. Three were out and waving as George slid by; they screamed and clawed and jumped. George took off fast.

Whatever kind of trip their driver was on, he still had hand and foot control. His lights picked George up again much too soon, seemed to be gaining on him. George was being slowed by a series of curves, which his lights revealed to the

107

driver in back, who probably was born on this road. Leaning hard when he reached a stretch, George flicked on the overhead light again. 115 to 120. Thank God he was carrying no wife or family on this trip, for he did not know if he would have dared drive this fast and well, and no doubt someone would have been screaming at him long ago. In fact the radio was screaming now, in raving dj voice. Something about an international gang of astrocosmonauts, if one could believe one's ringing ears. When the radio cut into the middle of a country tune, George turned it off. One world at a time! The crazy cowboys were almost at his side; he rolled down his window and flailed his arm at them. "Stay back, you dopes, stay *back!*" They hung in tight, though he was straight-legging the accelerator as hard as he could.

There were lights around the next bend, a town? A town! Signs spoke of lovely motels and restaurants, friendly Lions and Elks. Another said he would be rejoining the divided highway soon, and he slowed down. When the cowboys pulled abreast, he dropped back, hung onto their bumper whichever way they swung. Now they pulled over to the right going around the bend, suddenly all stiff-backed with civic pride and due respect. Sighting the divided highway with its limited access ramps fifty yards ahead, George held ever so slightly back, not enough to cause alarm among excitable boys. Thank God, they were taken in, or crazy optimists. As soon as their car passed the exit ramp, George stomped the accelerator and shot onto it, caught a glimpse of the cowboys alone out there, sliding sidewise to a screaming stop. Exit speed 15 mph—the Impala was doing at least four times that. Braking as much as he dared, he hit the unbanked turn in a groaning slide. The Impala quivered from front to back, then straightened out, cornering so beautifully that he could have cried with gratitude and relief.

Almost everyone else was sleeping. George had Main Street all to himself; even Joe's Cactus Bar looked dark. Turning onto an unlit residential street, he switched off his lights, felt everything but his eyes begin to relax. Breathing is beautiful! He looked for someone to tell that to. A nice peaceful little town when you finally got to it. These folk had elected a sheriff of the uninquisitive, unobtrusive sort. They probably slept with

108

their doors unlocked, trusting to God and those barking dogs to scare the cowboys off. He stopped with some other cars in front of a house whose first floor was bright, probably the local headquarters of Insomniacs Anonymous. "Thank you, old pal," he said, turning his motor off. "Let's cool awhile." He adjusted the mirror so that he could watch the dark street from a slouch.

His instinct was to resist the craving for a cigarette, a carry-over from other nights in another desert, spent in hiding from crazed cowboys in Junkers. *Pas des allumettes!* Aha, the Impala's lighter popped into mind; with that and a carefully cupped hand, he could at once indulge and conceal a bad habit. Had someone thought to install lighters in the ambulances of North Africa, what a saving in nicotine fits. Breathing is beautiful, almost as beautiful as cigarette smoke.

He had to give that up after a couple of puffs, for lights crept up on him from the direction of Main Street. Slouching lower in the seat, his hand at the ignition, he watched them approach. Either they had a familiar glare or he had become phobic toward lights. By now they had picked up the Impala's stripe, the low-slung bulge of his tanks. They speeded up, slowed, seemed ready to stop. No, now they chugged by, five or six heads wearing Indian hats. George sat up with a sigh. He smoked openly now, watching that beautiful station wagon pass out of sight. Then, turning on the radio, lighter and lights, he too moved out. It was eleven o'clock, time for some rock. The Impala still had one tank, he saw by the overhead light. Behind them was dark.

The southern edge of town became a blacktop road which soon became a dirt. He had brought no Arizona map, but it would have taken the latest satellite photographs to record his route tonight. (Phase Five did have a full-face moon and cloudless sky right here.) That dirt road became a desert trail, losing itself in Indian Country, its destination a haphazard hut or chicken coop, a barrel cactus or palo verde tree, a big old car abandoned after one last big push. Calling on Air Corps celestial navigation lore, George held to a southerly course, Polaris over his left shoulder, Betelgeuse and Orion's Belt tight ahead. Overhead laughed the moon; it was wearing an Abe Lincoln beard tonight. He checked his odometer now and then, dead reckoning. This was a good time and place to eat his last hard-boiled egg—calories and vitamins, Miriam, protein and salt, Irene. Oh for a quart of beer to wash that down, but the sheriff had finished off every drop for miles around.

They picked up a road again at Friendly Corners. Somewhere to the south lay Perhaps. (Miriam, remember that?) George read the radio beam from here on in, to acid rock. Out on highway 8, the cowboys had apparently given up, this far east at least. Well, it was twelve o'clock—sorry, Miriam!—and cowboys are not so finely trained as astrocosmonauts. They would be heading for the bunkhouse now, or sleeping in the car if their gas gave out, if not in jail. The Impala was running a little low; they cruised into Tucson at conservative speed plus ten. It was like rolling down from ten days on the reservation late at night, into Phoenix then, to spend the rest of the month in the office doing paperwork for the welfare of the State, twenty years ago. Twelve times he had made that run, before retreating with the loot to a ghost town halfway between the Phoenicians and the Navajos, six months of paperwork of his own. What parties those twelve had been—he and Miriam, one new baby in the house, beer and feast. Even now, their first nights were usually good. Memories like that made a man grow stiff, tonight somewhat guiltily. Leaving the highway, the Impala's needle quivering at E, he glided along the familiar sandy trail that led to the lovely, haphazard hut.

It was dark, of course, she had not known to leave a light on for him. This was hardly a setting for telegrams. Smiling he got out of the car and filled his lungs with moonlit desert air. The Chevy was parked beneath the tamarack tree, looking well if a little tired. Stepping lightly on the lean-to porch, he tapped their signal on the door. He held his breath for her dreamy, then he hoped joyous, "George?" There was no sound at all inside, not even the rustling sheets and creaking springs. He rapped and rattled the knob this time, "Miriam?" No, she would have been at the door by now. He should have kept his key. On the other hand, it was she who had suggested he leave that. The sand in front had been hosed down today—yesterday. On the east side of the house, she had watered the chives. The Volkswagon was in the lean-to garage, looking smug; he had imagined she had gone somewhere in that. The back door

110

of the house was locked from inside. Taking his screw driver from his bag, he removed the kitchen screen. She had remembered to leave the window unlatched, in case she forgot her key, and had left their handy bench nearby. Ah, she had painted that, dark green? Taking off his shoes, he climbed on, tossed those and his bag in first, then with one well-practiced boost was sitting cross-legged on the kitchen table like Gandhi home early from jail. "Hello? Hello? Mahatma's here!"

She had not left unexpectedly. Everything was more or less in place, the dishes washed but for one spoon and coffee cup, as though she had had a few minutes to herself after getting home from work. Had she had time to sit out on the porch, or watch the sun set on their vast backyard from her painted bench? Probably she had spent her time inside tonight, for there was more than one ring on the table top. Maybe her mother had come by for her. If a beau, that man was due for a surprise tonight. Not to seem to be hiding anything from anyone, George turned on all three lights in the house. Then he went to the refrigerator, turning on the fourth. In some ways she was leading an awfully temperate life; there were two little beers amid all the milk and pop. He hunted in vain for wine beneath the sink. Damn, if he had sent her a telegram she would have stocked plenty of each, perhaps baked a chicken for him. He could at least have written to tell her he would be stopping by one of these days, she might even have stayed home for him. No—in all fairness, maybe this beau was an important one.

She did have cold meats—and anchovies! He began his meal in the kitchen, after washing the dust and smoke from his mouth with two glasses of water. After midnight, three nights out, anchovies are at least as good as baked chicken, when washed down by a cold quart of milk. Sloshing contentedly, he carried the beers and meats to the front room. Everything was almost the same, changed if at all in little ways that he alone felt, the prints on the walls perhaps a little more faded, the upright piano perhaps a little more upright, the bed perhaps a little more chaste. She was still reading *Time*, passed down by her mother, and a few library books, one a Koestler that he had recently written her about. Seated in the easy chair beneath the lamp, he thumbed through a *Time* with last week's

111

moon on the cover. He finished both beers without discovering what they thought might become of that.

Given a few extra ounces of gas, an hour's extra time, he would have gone out for more beer. Maybe he would use the Chevy when Miriam got back, if she did. At 2:45? She seemed gone for the night. He had been looking forward, more than he had realized. It was a long time since they had had a talk. Maybe she would have heard some news, or would she still be quoting last week's editorial evasions? In any case, she would have her own news very well in mind, and he himself had lots to tell someone. He went over some of the highlights in his nodding head. Let her shake hers in disbelief of that! Yawning, crumpling his beer cans, he carried them to the paper bag beneath the sink. He rinsed his dish and glass, placed them on the drain beside her spoon and cup. Turning out the lights, he took off his fetid clothes and slipped between her clean sheets. On a trying journey it felt good to spend a night at home . . . Wake me, Miriam . . . Sweet dreams, Irene . . .

112

SIX

He awoke alone, after a complicated dream of wives, in which at least one of them had ended up satisfied. Now he satisfied himself. Probably it was just as well things had gone this way, made the chance of misunderstandings less. Travel always left him stiff. Afterward he lulled abed with a cigarette. Everything looked more usual today, with sunlight pouring in; the anemic prints absorbed it greedily. Even the piano seemed to try to make him feel at home. Up on his feet, George tickled it, then remade the bed. In the bathroom he shaved, brushed his teeth, and took a vigorous shower bath. Understandably she had adjusted the nozzle to her own taste, and he did not alter it.

He ate his own breakfast, bread, butter, milk, out on the bench. She had painted it dark green indeed, and with an habitual care. She had a beautiful concentration on things close to hand. The chollas looked very well, the mesquite and greasewood too. Leaning back, George basked a while in the sun, which was still ascending the startled, sparkling sky. Soon enough, he brushed his crumbs off Miriam's bench and replaced her screen, returned his glass to the sink. Now he went out to the tool shed for a piece of rubber hose and a gallon jug, retrieved from among many similar souvenirs. White Port was not his usual drink; he wondered if they had had any good times on that. The Chevy looked better in morning's light, and did not resent his taking a little of her juice. The parched Impala gurgled thanks. On his way back from the tool shed George watered the chives and where the herbs had been. After hosing his hands and rinsing his mouth, he sat down on the porch to write a note.

'Dear M, Sorry to have missed you—I didn't know ahead of time just when I'd be passing through, on my way East. The

113

place looks very nice, including the handsome bench. Excuse me, I had to siphon a gallon of the Chevy's gas to get my thirsty driveaway Impala (a race car—more of that in my next letter) to the nearest pump. The Chev still has plenty. I'm leaving you a copy of my new book by way of exchange. See you soon, or in Perhaps. Love, G.'

He inscribed the book to her with love. It was time to be hitting the sandy trail. They moved out slowly, not to waste gas or roll any sun-drenched lizards flat, and made it easily to a well-known pump. The boy, new to George, settled for the remainder of his ongone roll and most of the remnants of his original stake. He still had plenty of phone change though, and thought to reassure himself before quitting town.

"Yes?"

"Hello—Bertha?"

"Yes."

"This is George Alberts. How are you doing?"

"All right."

"And Mike?"

"All right. Yourself?"

"Fine! I'm just passing through town. I stopped at the house last night and found Miriam not at home . . ."

"Oh, she's gone to a retreat down south—with Pat Henderson and some others."

"I suppose she'll be gone all weekend?"

"Oh yes—until sometime tomorrow, I think she said."

"Well, I left her a note, but give her my love when you see her, will you?"

"Oh yes."

"And good luck to you and Mike."

"Oh you too," Bertha said.

It was time they left. They drove glumly through the gaudy parts, out into the almost limited desert east. The radio said those cowboys had finally rolled their vehicle, a stolen one, at midnight on Highway 8; two of them had been apprehended by the sheriff, at the hospital. Here was a new-laid stretch, and the Impala seemed pleased with it, seemed not to mind the fresh-tarred access roads and parking lots, the immobile homes propped on sleazy cinder blocks. Here and there a forlorn house stood in the midst, with a dessicated tree,

114

a barn, the ghost of a chicken coop. Somewhere, on barn or tree, usually hung a rusty, heart-broken barrel hoop, the ring of sand beneath trod long ago. What kind of shape were those boys in now; how were their sons doing in the uniformed Little Leagues? Nice work, Bertha: I see your Real Estate. Oh you too, yourself. Well, at least he hadn't mentioned the smug VW she bought Miriam when he left, nor the plots she was staking out in their vast backyard.

He tried to remember how this stretch had looked two years ago when he was heading east, but memory blurred that with other trips. Probably he had not studied the scenery so closely that day, with Miriam left behind in tears, New York ahead. He was not unused to making trips alone, of course; but strange it had been after twenty close family years to find oneself all at once moving through life *alone*. Strange heading "home" to a city he had done no more than visit off and on for thirty years, peopled no longer with relatives and friends but commandeered by migrant publishers and movie men who thought of his books, and him, as pawn and property. Not surprising that he had dawdled on that trip, stopping at Lordsburg to buy and mail Janet some birthday herbs, stopping at Las Cruces that first night to look for girls in a hard-cocked, half-hearted way. He had spent the night alone in a motel they had stopped at more than once on their ways to Mexico, and with crackers and beer, reminisced himself to sleep. At least there had still been some kind of news on TV and radio, less musak too. He could remember following the hourly plays and ploys, framing his analyses of them for an imaginary, comprehending Miriam. Too late now for even that. The sallow moon had decided to stay up all day, clean-shaven and smiling enigmatically. Did it like what it saw these days? Probably there had been more freedom and privacy in Arizona 1950 than there was now in the Northwest Territories and Antarctica. In fact, for all the capitains, Junkers, and mortar shells, he had felt more freedom with the British and French in North Africa, 1942-3, than he had in their homelands in 1970-1. Northern Idaho 1959 was about equal to northern British Columbia 1968; southern British Columbia 1969 was *circa* Seattle '65. Poor Australasia. Poor Golan Heights. Poor Yucatan. Look hard, moon. The earth, as a physical object, is still, I imagine, one of the most attractive beings in this universe.

They were in the eastern Arizona heights, heading for Lordsburg and its well-known Woolworth herbal shop, heading for the Land of Enchantment, Janet's native state. At the border line they bade greetings and farewells. Hello, Road Forks! See you anon, Gila monsters! We're heading for the Great Divide! It was in those mountains, a few miles north, that they had camped one summer month awaiting a thousand dollars from Hollywood, a six months' pass to Mexico. Without a tent, they had slept in the car whenever the tarp got drenched. Much of their daytime had been spent chipping foul words off the Forest Service rocks. On the last possible day the option renewal had been withheld. *Shit.* They had struck their sodden tarp, headed for Albuquerque and the OEO. Four months of that had earned him six months and half a novel in Mexico. Running out of Old Mexican time, he had finished the last few pages in New, in a ghost town rife with bugs. Phase Four underwent basic training there.

It was starting to rain. Well-timed today for once. Let it rain, let it slosh—no need for an Impala wash. He had not checked his contract for cleanliness yet, but it was always better to deliver in rain, sleet, or snow, that way the question did not come up. Frightful weather, isn't it! Yes, heavenly! There came to mind another rain, less fortuned, that had befallen Phoenix a few years ago. Their first afternoon in town, he had gone to the ball park to hustle some money for dinner that night. After two hungry hours in the Concessions room, word had leaked down that they were calling it off. George had gone home with a bag of salted nuts, not trusting those beers to a thin summer shirt. Cheer up though, they had scheduled a double header the next afternoon, what a feast there had been *that* night! It all works out.

Or used to do. In Las Cruces the sun and the moon were out, that rain had not washed the car but pocked its dirt. The contract made no mention of cleanliness; it was a question of conscience and pocketbook. After counting his change, George called the boss, a Mr. Henry Oberland.

"Hello, this is George Alberts. I'm delivering your car from—"

"Yes, bring it right over, will you. We're ten miles south or east on 10, turn left at the yellow light. The gate will open itself for you. We're the big greystone house, on the left, you'll know it by the cross on top. All right?"

"I wond—"

"Yes thanks very much."

He got out his map. Ah yes, *entendu*. Thanks very much. The Impala had, if any, just that many southeasterly miles left in her, so he pulled up to a pump with an old old man in front.

"Excuse me, I just want a quarter's worth—I'm delivering this car and I don't want—"

"I understand, I understand." And pumped his half-pint with a truly wondrous care, delivering each precious drop.

"Thank you, sir!"

"Thank *you*, young man!"

With a send-off like that, he was in a mood to jump the fence into Mexico. With Irene and two tanks of gas, he imagined himself making a run for it. Chihuahua, here we come! No, the Impala loomed too conspicuous. Besides, Mr. Oberland seemed to have immediate need of it. They slowed at the yellow light, turned onto the asphalt lane leading to the limited access gate. That electronic marvel swung open without creak or clank, and they headed for church. There were no other cars in the parking lot, but this was Saturday after all, and there were yellow lines enough to warm a bishop's heart. The plywood sign above the oaken and wrought-iron doors read CRUX DELIVERIES THIS DOOR ONLY—Salesmen and Visitors Use Pastor's Entrance in Rear, so he followed the arrows there. A yellowing card tacked near that door said BELL OUT OF ORDER KNOCK. George tapped, one-knuckled, between the studs. Inside, a motor whirred on, whirred off.

"Coming! Coming! Coming!"

She flung open the door and stood shaking her grey head at him, her yellowing apron caught up in her wringing hands. "Everything happens in threes!" she said.

"Doesn't it!"

She didn't need him to tell her that. "Oh, come in and sit down!" she said. "He's in the Study. He'll be out in a little bit."

"Fine! Thanks!" George said, sitting down on what looked

like a sawed-off pew, cushioned in deep red velveteen, its brass studs worn shiny smooth. With the door flung closed, she herself looked almost contemporary in the mellow electric light of the vestibule. Other than the pew, there were just he, she, and the Persian rug. From behind the Study door, level male voices could be heard over the whine of her Electrolux. Her "little bit" was heading toward eternity.

"Watch those feet!" she cried, charging him from across the room. "Sorry!" he said, all athwart on the pew.

"Martha, turn that damn thing off." In contrast, this man was all of one cool, short-sleeved piece. *Damn* did not raise his voice. He had near perfect hair, on a clean young head. In fact his only obvious flaw was a lack of irregularity, neither side of his face could have been the better one. "Oberland. Come in, Alberts. You had an easy trip."

"Oh yes."

"The Impala's in good shape."

"Marvelous."

The Study had been modernized, bathed in shimmering neon light. The desk was a drafting board, a computer stood where the lampstand had probably been. The lowboy had been replaced by a stereo console system, topped by the TV and radio. Cassettes and cartridges lined the floor-to-ceiling shelves, carrying out the decor of the Venetian blinds. "Have a seat," Oberland said, indicating a stool on wheels. "Sherry?"

"Yes. Thanks very much."

"There's white port too, but . . ."

"Sherry's fine."

Pouring sherry for both of them, the host rolled over to George on his own stool, a higher one. "Here's to Rollins Dolphin," he said, and winked, or rather blinked.

"You know of them?"

"Oh sure. How is Los Angeles looking these days?"

"Fantastic!"

"Yes, I used to live there myself." He restrained a smile, but George sensed that it would have been a perfect one. "You only stayed there about a day this trip."

"Quite long enough."

"You did get along well with the dolphin though."

"Well . . ."

"Yes, I could tell." He checked a sheet of paper on the drafting board. "You've been living in Tacoma recently. Lay Reader for Special Classes. Good old Gleb, etc. How does all that go?"

"That goes." George offered his host a cigarette, though he knew it would be refused. Under a tolerant scrutiny, he lit one for himself. "You mentioned Rollins Dolphin just now. How do you happen to know of them?"

Oberland waved a hand at the crowded room, not so much vaguely as conclusively. "You can kiss all that goodbye in any case. Once again. That gag writer—Whatsisname?—has already made a film of your book himself, you know. The one who had an option just before you joined the OEO?"

"Yes . . ."

Oberland glanced at his drawing board. "We were talking about Tacoma. You and your family once lived here in New Mexico."

"Yes."

"With the OEO you were a Work Training Specialist."

"Right."

"Yes, that's when I first picked you up. Then you ran off to Mexico."

"Well, yes . . ."

"Wrote your fifth novel there."

"Mainly, yes."

"After that you were in Silverton, Phoenix, and northern Idaho."

"Right."

"You spent the winter of '68-'69 in Canada."

"Yes."

"Caretaking a Lutheran summer camp."

"Good enough." Apologias, Pappa John.

"Then you and your family made that trip to Europe on the Happer advance. Twenty-five hundred, I think."

"Yes."

Oberland checked his drafting board, checked again. "England, by way of Mexico?"

"We were heading for Central America. Our car broke down."

"You and your wife separated soon after you got back. We didn't think you ever would."

119

"Nor did I until a few years ago."

"You went to New York for about a year and a half."

"Right."

"Worked as a messenger."

"Yes."

"There are some gaps. Where were you working at the beginning and end of that?"

"Here and there, all over town."

"Ah." Oberland jotted something down. "Then you went to Florida."

"Correct."

"Let's get back to New Mexico." Oberland cleared his throat, while flicking a switch behind his back. "More sherry, George?"

"Thank you."

The gracious host sniffed his own. He seemed to try not to look at George too levelly, in vain of course. "Drugs, hypnotism, subliminals—you saw all that in the OEO."

"Oh yes."

"That was a bad session. Yours was one of two brains that wouldn't work right."

"Yes, I know."

"Odd, the social worker type is usually more dependable than that."

"I'm not a type."

"Oh, that's right." Oberland touched George's knee. For a few seconds he seemed to contemplate. "Hey, I'll never forget old Martinez striking his head with his fist that last day!"

"Neither will I!"

"You were making your parting remarks about not having received the official word from Santa Fe—about the proper disposal of your manual."

"I remember, yes."

Oberland rocked gently on his stool, breathing his sherry, probably smiling to himself. "That was a funny one," he said. "You heard the other dissident person—Baxter—was sent to Lubbock for further training?"

"I guessed as much."

"George, where are you headed now?"

"I was thinking of New York," George said, "but now I'm not entirely sure."

Nodding, Oberland consulted his sheet again. "Your Happers book was remaindered recently—you're following that one up?"

"I'm following all of them up."

"Your Happer editor-person—Nanny?"

"Nikki."

"Oh?" He made a note of that. "She keeps in good close touch: date of 'publication,' total number of copies, names of those ordering, number if any of orders filled, that sort of thing. She's an extremely efficient person, as you know. Has an extremely interesting collection of writers too," he added with a little bow. "The only trouble she's had at all was with the Mao poems—he insisted on a first printing of two hundred twenty million. It presented a real logistical problem, I can tell you. We've got a few million of them boarded up in the clerestory right now, but that's all right, they're moving well." Going to the computer, he slid in a card, waited, read. "Yes." Back on his stool, he studied George. "Where were we, George?"

"Well, I was wondering about the bookstores, how a book gets moving well."

"Oh. Well, in a case like that the salesmen simply swamp the stores, promising lavish promotion too. You've seen the ads—'Fifty Thousand copies sold in Hackensack.' Then it helps to give the author as much TV exposure as possible—by satellite if necessary (in this case, the President handled that himself). From then on, conditioned nature takes its course—a book moves well. For example, I don't remember ever seeing you, do I—on a commercial channel, I mean."

"Oh no."

"Exactly. Of course, there are other factors involved—I oversimplify. Salesmen have many wiles. Of course the Printers and Packers League is very well-integrated too. The Writers League has been thoroughly infiltrated, as you must know. Then of course we have the International Pent-up League— that was effected through the translators, mainly. The Reviewers are the tricky ones, they'll come up with a natural response sometimes. Naturally we try to keep books away from them—their review copies are lost in the mails, misdirected to the ladies clubs, etc. Whenever one does write a good review, we simply move the movers in on him, gobble any follow-up—

you've noticed that. The bad reviewers—they're already ours. The Agents are a big help of course."

"Yes, that's why I handle all that myself."

"Nanny *is* your agent—she sold you out. We take care of the English Professors too, of course, that's easy enough. Grants, tenure, sabbaticals in Singapore, all that manure. By the way, Professor Jemmings left a message for you: he's doing industrial research in Missoula—stop by and see him if you're out that way."

"Thanks. I'm apt to pass through Missoula pretty fast. I did slow down for Los Angeles."

"Speaking of Los Angeles, you've seen our new magazines, *Thus* and *So*?"

"I've glanced at them."

"They're moving well, especially *So*. We're developing a pretty good chain of them, from the Scottish Highlands to Tokyo and beyond. Their sucking the English language up like a vacuum."

"*Why?*"

"Nothing personal." He waved his hand at the room again. "All this has but one competitor left, you know. The written language can still be dangerous. On the other hand, if properly confined it can be most useful too. The goal is ISOFOL—"

There was a rap on the door and a large man sidled in, dressed in the inconspicuous garb of a deacon or bodyguard. Inspecting George with grey, expressionless eyes, he handed a card to Oberland.

"Hold it, Porter," Oberland said, reading the card. "All right. Good. Thanks. You can get back to work."

Nodding, the man sidled out and closed the door.

"Nice job, George." Inclining his head, Oberland seemed almost to smile.

"Sir?"

"You delivered everything not only in time but in A-1 shape."

"The Impala, you mean?"

"That too, but I was speaking of freight."

"Freight? I thought the trunk was empty except for spare tire and tools."

Oberland chuckled dryly now. "Oh, the trunk. You didn't

122

happen to look in the left gas tank? No? We have a gasproof compartment in there for storing cards and tapes. You probably noticed your mileage falling off toward the end of each run?"

"As a matter of fact I did."

"Tapeworming, we call that—a little joke." It cracked his face. "Now, can I be of any further help?"

"Well, I was wondering—the cowboys were a random event?"

"The cowboys?"

"Four or five of them chased me in a race car in southern Arizona last night."

"Hm. I would guess so, yes. Let me check on that." He got to his feet, stepped to a door. "We keep that one in the pantry—it's fourth generation, you see. I'll be right back." He was, with a scrap of tape. "We have no background on that," he said. "It qualifies as a natural phenomenon. Conditions in southern Arizona were favorable for such as that last night. The phenomenon occurred somewhere in the vicinity of Maricopa, I suspect."

"Pretty close."

"Yes, conditions were very favorable. Let me show you some statistics on that." Oberland opened the door to the vestibule, led George across the immaculate Persian rug to a larger door. Somewhere on high whined a vacuum. Oberland slammed the door on it, waved a hand at the vaulted interior of the church. "We keep Phase Six univacs in the nave," he said. One in the pulpit too. "This way we can keep on top of the trends. Note they run sequentially, by state. There's Arizona over there, near the apse," burning bright. Each state had its own panel of flashing numbers, like miniature election or market boards. "Yes, Maricopa was hot last night. We program a number of variable factors: murders, rapes, muggings, drug abuses, marriage dissolutions, car thefts, police brutalities, voluntary institutionalizations, Valium and Librium sales, Prolixin dosages, bootlegged nuclear arms, faggots and dike chauvinists seized, student papers, etc., etc., in addition to the unobservable entities. When an area approaches forty percent ideal saturation, we know we have it softened up. Take Los Angeles there, for your current optimum. You'll note

123

Oregon is weak, Idaho very weak. Nevada's always strong. Texas comes and goes. Oklahoma 50-50, like Iowa. Minnesota weak—they're having a severe cold spell there of course. Minneapolis-St. Paul looks promising though. We'll just have to shift a little more pressure there, from Milwaukee-Madison probably—you can see that."

"Oh yes."

"Chicago will take care of itself. New York is a strange one, isn't it? Well, Phoenix at least is won. Isn't Miami hot tonight! New Orleans is high. Look at North Carolina coming on! What we count on is fragmented personalities getting *together*—the assimilation of seeking depersonalization, what the Church used to call demoralization. Do you follow? . . . Are you listening?"

"Yes!" George's glance had drifted up to the clerestory, where stars twinkled tamely in a captive sky. "You keep your eye on all that as well?"

"Oh yes. That's easier—not so many known variables. Of course, there's no collating the unobservables."

"Wasn't there some excitement up there last night?"

"Excitement? Oh, you mean the Moon!" Oberland chuckled hollowly, shook his head. "That gang really thought they had it for a while. Don't worry though, everything's under complete control. You can see by looking at her, how warm she glows. We're shifting some of the pressure now to Mars—" a wave of his hand dismissed all that—"Let's get down to Earth again. I imagine you're a little tired. You did get some sleep along the way?"

"Oh yes!"

"Not much that first night, I estimate—in North California."

"Well, no . . ." You get your sleep, young man!

"That old hag was a real bore, wasn't she?"

"Well . . ."

"Hey, you know her granddaughter—Belle? She's been lost since we set that computed boy on her in Grand Rapids, MI."

"Aha."

"Your Janet is in Saskatchewan, you know."

"I know."

"Your Irene is going to be an unusually fine poet, by the way."

124

"I know that too!"

"Yes, yes—just trying to be friendly, George. Can I be of any further help?"

"Let's worry about the girl in the D.V.E. trailer—Noxzema, the lady called her—I don't know what her real name was."

"I'll check on it—that's in the baptistry." He was gone a bit longer this time—is it only imagination that paints Mars so red?—and came back bearing a scrap of tape, rather limp. "Melanie De La Ponce. She's lost," he said, dropping the tape in a chalice. "What's your secret, George?"

"My what?"

"You seem to have a prescience that sees you through, or a clairvoyance that intercepts an unusual number of energies or messages."

"It sometimes seems so, yes."

"We normally handle such types—excuse me, individuals —in more direct ways. For example, we have medicines now that can desex a man in twenty months. We can induce cancer in twentyfive. You seem to be stubborn in these ways too."

"Oh yes. Now may I ask you one?"

"Please do."

George waved a hand at the nave and the apse, the pulpit, the clerestory. "What do you hope to accomplish with all this?"

For the first time, perhaps in his life, Oberland grinned, quite flawlessly. "Pow-er," he said.

"One more: why are you telling me all this?"

"I'm an anarchist."

It was 20:55 Mountain Time, according to the altarpiece. "One more?"

"Shoot."

"Have you got a telephone I can use?"

"Hm, I think I can arrange it, yes . . . It's in the hall." He led George out there, to a telephone hanging on the wall beneath the stairs. A man of average height, he had to stand on his toes for it. It had a handle, which he cranked. He jiggled the cradle hard. "Operator! . . . Operator!"

George was counting his change when Oberland turned to him. "George, don't worry about that—we'll charge it to the Church . . . Hold on, Operator! . . . Here you go—you may have to shout!"

125

The operator was shouting too. "What! What!"
George counted the number out.
"What state is that?"
"Washington."
"Washing *what?*"
"WA! WA!"
"Well, I'll try!" she cried.
"Thanks!"
The phone rang scarce half a ring. "Hello, I love you!"
"Yes, I you too! How are you?"
"Fine! I miss you! How and where are you?"
"Fine and in New Mexico. I miss you too!"
"What happened last night around ten o'clock?"
"You know about that?"
"Yes. Did you let me know that everything was all right at three o'clock?"
"Three o'clock? . . . Yes, I guess I did. Our circles are intertwining well! I'll tell you all about it when I get home. What's new with you?"
"Patter is pregnant!"
"You're kidding!"
"No, kittying—she's *fat!*"
"Wonderful! What else is new?"
"You got a thousand dollar check from Rollins Dolphin. Shall I read you his note?"
"Do."
"DEAR GEORGE. TERRIFIC WORKING WITH YOU. BEAUTIFUL. WE'VE GOT IT MADE. BEST."
Best *what,* for God's sake. "Has there been anything else?"
"A contract from a lawyer in Hollywood—Harry Hearst."
"How does it look?"
"Wow. You'll have to try to read it for yourself."
"Yes. Nothing else?"
"He sent a bill with it, for two hundred bucks."
"Ow wow. What else?"
"Your three minutes is up!"
"Operator, hold off a while!"
"Signal when you're done!"
"I will!"
"George?"

126

"Yes! What else?"

"Did you see Miriam?"

"She wasn't home. I stayed at the house last night."

"Oh, good."

He laughed. "I thought you'd approve of that."

"Where are you going next?"

He paused, and then, "Home," he said.

"Right away?"

Oberland handed George a scrap of tape: I CAN GET YOU AN EXPENSES PAID CAR TO SEATTLE. "Yes, right away. I have a book to write and, excuse me, Operator, a wife to fuck."

It was Irene who pretended to gasp, and laughed. "Speaking of that, last night I dreamt that I was pregnant too. It's not true, of course."

"Well, throw away the goop."

"You're serious?"

"Yes. Aren't you?"

"*Yes*. Hurry home—safely."

"Don't worry about that."

"Shall I wire you some money?"

"They say it's an expenses-paid car—I'll see how it goes. Don't worry, please."

They kissed.

"*Us*."

"Yes, all of *us*." He waited for Irene to hang up. "Operator?"

Oberland reached for the phone. "I'll take care of that. You *are* a stubborn one, aren't you, George?"

"Oh yes. Now that I know the ground rules, I can't wait to start all over again."

Oberland managed to arch one eyebrow. "How will you do it this time?"

George smiled. "The same old way," he said, "naturally." He counted his change. He was ready to go. If things got tight, he could always stop off in Oregon for his Trojan quarter.

127

Printed February 1977 in Santa Barbara & Ann Arbor
for the Black Sparrow Press by Mackintosh and Young
& Edward Brothers Inc. This edition is published in
paper wrappers; there are 200 hardcover copies
numbered & signed by the author; & 26 copies
handbound in boards by Earle Gray lettered &
signed by the author.

Douglas Woolf was born in Manhattan
        in 1922. Life
                continues
wieldy.
        Time strains
                itself. Birds
feather the weather.
Suns
        weld
                space.